She hardly felt Dan lift her into the passenger seat. He stood in the open door.

"You can get through this," he said. "Squeeze my hands."

She tried, but her body seemed to have no will of its own. It was as if her mind was imprisoned somewhere dark and terrifying.

"We'll do it together." He squeezed her fingers for a slow count of five and then relaxed.

After several moments of the gentle pressure to her hands, she was able to squeeze back. Her breaths became less shuddering, and she grew aware of her surroundings. The late afternoon sun poked through the clouds, outlining Dan's strong shoulders, and revealed his look of concern tinged with quiet confidence.

You can get through this.

She continued to breathe and squeeze until she could get the words out, a stumbling gush of details that made his face go from concerned to enraged.

"I am going to see that guy in prison if it's the last thing I ever do on this planet."

Dana Mentink is an award-winning author of Christian fiction. Her novel *Betrayal in the Badlands* won a 2010 RT Reviewers' Choice Best Book Award, and she was pleased to win the 2013 Carol Award for *Lost Legacy*. She has authored more than a dozen Love Inspired Suspense novels. Dana loves feedback from her readers. Contact her via her website at danamentink.com.

Books by Dana Mentink

Love Inspired Suspense

Pacific Coast Private Eyes

Dangerous Tidings
Seaside Secrets

Wings of Danger

Hazardous Homecoming
Secret Refuge

Stormswept

Shock Wave
Force of Nature
Flood Zone

Treasure Seekers

Lost Legacy
Dangerous Melody
Final Resort

Visit the Author Profile page at Harlequin.com for more titles.

SEASIDE SECRETS

DANA MENTINK

HARLEQUIN® LOVE INSPIRED® SUSPENSE

Recycling programs
for this product may
not exist in your area.

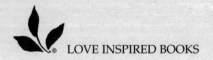

LOVE INSPIRED BOOKS

ISBN-13: 978-0-373-67751-1

Seaside Secrets

www.Harlequin.com

Printed in U.S.A.

I am the vine; you are the branches.
If you remain in Me and I in you, you will bear much fruit;
apart from Me you can do nothing.
—*John* 15:5

To those who struggle with PTSD and those who help them overcome, blessings on you and yours.

ONE

The sound exploded through the crowded street. Angela Gallagher screamed, jerking so violently she stepped wrong off the curb and sprawled onto the asphalt. Her purse flew out of her grip. On hands and knees, she struggled for breath, pulse thundering as her senses tried to right themselves.

The worker who had dropped the empty pallet went about his unloading, oblivious to the panic he'd caused in one out-of-control woman. "Get up," she told herself furiously.

A hand grasped her elbow, a middle-aged man with salt-and-pepper hair and a wide face. He wore khakis and a plaid shirt. His eyes were flat, probing. "Are you all right?"

She swallowed a surge of panic. *Not every stranger is dangerous. You're not in a war zone anymore.* A deep breath in and out. "Yes, thank you." She forced a smile. "I wasn't watching my step."

Why did he want to know? *It's called polite small talk.* Paranoia. She could not get rid of it, no matter how hard she poured herself into Bible study or prayer.

"Meeting someone here at the wharf," she said.

He stooped to help as she retrieved the spilled items from her purse. "Bad time for that. During Beach Fest the whole town is nuts. Where were you supposed to meet?"

"Oh, somewhere around here. I'll find him. Thanks for your concern." She gave him another smile and edged away, toward the vendors.

"I could help, if you'd like."

"No. No, thanks."

He studied her face. A moment too long? "Enjoy your stay, Miss Gallagher," he said softly, turning away into the crowd.

Goose bumps prickled her skin. One more look, soft and sly, and he was gone.

For a moment, she felt frozen, paralyzed. Her name. How had he known? Her brain slowly began to reboot. Her wallet. He'd picked it up for her. It had probably fallen open and he'd read her driver's license. *What is the matter with you?* she asked herself. He was a regular guy, offering help, and this was not wartime, not here.

A bead of sweat trickled down Angela's back, at odds with the chill ocean air. The press of the crowd overwhelmed her senses. She had not imagined when she'd made the eight-hour drive from Coronado to Monterey that she would land in the middle of some sort of festival. Would she have come if she had known? *No*, her gut said. *Yes*, her heart corrected.

People walked along Fisherman's Wharf, stopping at the craft booths and trailing down to the rocky shore to watch the kayakers and the whale-watching boats chugging through the choppy waters of California's central coast. The January cold pressed in; she gathered her jacket around her. Where was he? He was supposed to meet her under the balloon arch a half hour ago. Blowing on her fingers, she scanned the wharf again. Though she'd never clapped eyes on Tank Guzman, she knew exactly what he would look like. His identical twin, Julio, had died in her arms from sniper bullets meant for her. Again Julio's gentle face rose up in her mind, the sweet hopes he'd shared about a life with his girlfriend upon his return from Afghanistan, the easy banter that was a salve to the tension of the war.

"Chaplain," he'd told her with an irrepressible grin, "you've got the hardest job in the navy. All I gotta do is keep you alive, but you have to tend to all the wandering souls in this unit."

Yet Julio Guzman, a chaplain's assistant and her bodyguard, had been the one to die. He sacrificed his life for hers, a navy chaplain serving in a combat zone without so much as a handgun in her possession. She tried to bring herself back to the present.

Vendors clustered under white tents in the street, offering samples and calling to potential customers.

Noise, colors, smells and sounds assaulted her. As if by some inner compass, she found herself moving away from the crowd down toward the crashing surf, forcing herself to hold her gait to a stroll instead of an outright sprint. The beach offered some respite. There were people exploring the sand and the tide pools nestled in the clefts of rock. Children squealed, peering at the little hermit crabs and tiny fish inhabiting the crevices. She remembered doing the same with her father, but instead of the tingle of nostalgia, she felt nothing but cold. Sucking in deep breaths of sea-scented air, she moved away from the people, seeking the solace of a nearly empty stretch of beach.

One more look back. The man with the khaki pants had not appeared on the warped stairs that led down to the beach. *You see? Paranoia, Angie.* It's what her three sisters would have said back before they'd lost their private investigator father to a murderer. Now they were less innocent, more cynical, having decided to keep their father's private investigation office going. And she, struggling and desperate to reclaim her life, had signed on as a woefully underqualified part-time investigator.

So why hadn't she told them about the case she was working on now? Finding Tank Guzman, Julio's errant brother.

Because it's not a case. She lifted her face in the direction of the surf. *It's personal.*

For the first time, she noticed a woman with a long black braid standing near her almost at the edge of the water. Angela was about to retreat, to find another solitary section of sand, when she heard the woman say, "No way, Tank."

Angela stiffened. Her imagination again? Had she heard right?

"Listen, I mean it," she said into her cell phone. "It's a bad idea. It's too dangerous. I told you to call it off, but I know you're going to go through with it anyway and get us both killed."

She really had said Tank. Angela stood frozen, blinking in surprise.

"My tire," she was saying. "No, it wasn't an accident." She looked around. "He might be watching us right now. Get out of here and go home. I'm going to do the same. Please, I'm begging you." Another long pause. "I'm sorry, Tank. I can't help. Please just let it go." She clicked off the phone.

Angela felt as if her body were acting under the orders of someone else. "Excuse me," she said.

The woman whirled so fast her foot slipped, and she went down on her knee.

"I'm sorry," Angela started, reaching out a hand to her. "I heard you say Tank."

"Back off," the woman said.

"I need to find Tank. Where is he?"

"I said, stay away." She pulled something from her jacket pocket.

Angela gaze went to the knife in the woman's hand.

The weapon was small, barely bigger than the woman's shaking palm. Angela was frozen to the spot. "I'm trying to find a man named Tank Guzman."

The woman's eyes widened to black pools. "Why?"

The wind whipped Angela's chin-length bob of brown hair around her face, stinging her eyes. "I know...I knew his brother. We arranged a meeting. Here. But he didn't show."

"His brother." Something shimmered in her expression as she said the words. "So you're the person from Pacific Coast Investigations?"

Angela tried not to show her surprise. "Yes. I overheard your call. You don't want Tank to meet with me. Why?"

In an instant, the woman was edging away. "Never mind. Listen to me. Tank was wrong to contact you. There's nothing going on here. It was a mistake."

Terror reflected in the woman's eyes.

Angela hoped she could force out a calm tone. "I can see you're scared. I'm a navy chaplain. Maybe I can help."

The woman started. "A navy chaplain? I thought you were an investigator."

"My family owns an investigation firm, but I'm a chaplain first and foremost." *At least, I used to be.*

A bitter smile twisted the woman's lips. "Then you'd better start praying, because Tank isn't going to be alive for very long. And if you get involved with him—" she shook her head "—you won't, either."

Dan Blackwater remembered vehicles, makes and models, headlights and license plates. Mechanically, he scanned the parking lot, making mental notes. Since Afghanistan, he'd been forced to notice things, tiny things out of place, little details that could mean something was about to blow up. Something as simple as a soda can in an odd place could preclude a rain of fire and a parade of injuries. Now he couldn't seem to unlearn the habit. He blinked hard. *You're here now, in Cobalt Cove.* He sucked in a huge breath of ocean air. He was home, thank God. Mostly, anyway.

As he jogged toward the beach, carrying the bag Lila had left at the clinic, cutting through the parking area to avoid the crowds, he noted her Camry in the jammed lot. He'd gotten to know that car pretty well when he helped fix her flat hours before at the clinic. Their shifts overlapped sometimes, at the tiny building on the outskirts of town where he volunteered his surgical services stitching up wounds and arranging help for those living on the fringes of society. Lila worked there as a paid employee, a dental hygienist for those who needed one.

They'd chatted about her plans to go to the Beach Festival on her way home from work, but she hadn't seemed very excited about the prospect. More nervous really, so nervous she'd left without the tote bag she carried everywhere with her. Odd. But people were odd, no two the same, except in some universal ways he'd noted in his time as a heart surgeon at the NATO hospital in Afghanistan. They all loved, laughed and died in pretty much the same ways.

His phone rang, pulling him from his thoughts. He answered. "Blackwater."

"You missed another one."

"I called and canceled."

His physical therapist sighed heavily into the phone. Dan could picture Jeb Paulson's fleshy face scowling in disapproval, eyebrows like two grizzled caterpillars crawling across his forehead.

"The rehabilitation window is closing, Dr. Blackwater. If you don't take your rehab seriously, you'll never return to the operating room."

I don't want to return to an operating room. "I'm happy with what I'm doing now."

"Puttering around in boats? You can't be serious. You're the best heart surgeon in the country."

"Flattery. And it's kayaks, not boats. You should try it, Jeb. It would relax you."

"Having you come to your appointments would

relax me. I'm scheduling you for Monday noon. If you don't show, I'm saddling up Old Lucy and coming after you."

He grinned. Old Lucy was Jeb's ancient motorcycle, circa 1949. "That I'd like to see."

"Monday," Jeb said before disconnecting.

Dan stowed his phone and flexed his hand. It still ached a bit from his bicycle crash on his last race along the coast a month before. *Too fast, too tight a turn*, his brain had screamed, but the rush of adrenaline proved more powerful. Until he'd flown over the handlebars and skidded along the roadbed. Too bad he hadn't won the race before he crashed, he thought with a grin. When he flexed his fingers, they were only a little sore, slightly stiff, but little and slightly wouldn't do for a surgeon.

The window is closing...

Jeb was right. "I'll make it to the Monday appointment," he murmured to himself as he took off toward the beach, hoping to spot Lila along the way. He didn't. Slowing when he reached the top of the rickety wooden steps that led down to the sand, he edged over as he heard footsteps moving quickly up the warped slats.

Lila appeared, mouth open, hair wild. She gaped when she saw him.

"Dr. Blackwater. What are you doing here?"

"You left this at the clinic." He handed her the bag. "What's going on? You look scared."

"Never mind. I've gotta go. Thanks for bringing

me my stuff." She darted past him just as another woman reached the top step.

A shock ran through him as he took in her tall frame, the delicate curve of her mouth and cheek. He was back in Kandahar, Afghanistan, delivering devastating news to a young woman, holding her hands as she crumpled to the floor, advising her to take deep breaths as she hovered on the brink of passing out. Her eyes, misty green, had lingered in his memory throughout his transition to civilian life. Those green eyes regarded him now, and she stopped so abruptly she had to grab on to the railing for balance. Her swirl of dark hair was damp from the fog, curling in the barest of waves around her face. Her body was slimmer, her face a touch gaunt, he thought.

"I don't remember your last name," he said. "But I think your first name is Angela."

Her lips quivered. "The hospital," she said quietly. "You were a surgeon."

"Still am, at least on paper. Dan Blackwater. And you're Angela…"

"Gallagher."

"Navy chaplain."

A shadow of a smile. "At least on paper."

He could see the perspiration on her temple now, the shallow breathing, tense shoulders that told him their encounter was not welcome. Made sense. He represented her darkest hour; at least he hoped it was her darkest. Civilian life had to be easier than what she'd endured, if she really had been able to leave it behind. He remembered certain details now. Navy Chaplain Angela Gallagher brought in with minor wounds along with her chaplain's assistant, who had died from the bullets that tore through his aorta when he'd shielded her. God's handiwork ripped to irreparable shreds by the merciless progress of metal and machine.

"I need to find someone," she said, keeping a distance between them as she passed him.

"Lila?"

Angela started. "The woman who just ran up these stairs. Is that her name?"

He nodded. "She's a dental hygienist. She works at the same health clinic where I volunteer."

Angela's gaze shifted as she thought it over. "I've got to talk to her."

"She didn't look in the talking mood."

"I got that sense, too, when she pulled a knife."

Now it was his turn to gape. "What?"

"I've got to go."

"Bad idea. She's got a knife and you don't…"

She stiffened. "Carry a weapon?"

It wasn't what he'd meant, but her reaction stopped him cold, her expression brittle as glass.

"You're right, Dr. Blackwater. I don't."

The landing at the top of the stairs emptied out onto a cement sidewalk that led to the boardwalk. The crowds were thicker now, the lights in restaurant windows were advertising the beginning of the dinner hour. Paper lanterns that lined the sidewalks glowed in soft hues. While Dan struggled to think of how in the world he should handle the bizarre situation, Angela simply jogged by him and into the milling group.

Lila had pulled a knife on someone? The soft-spoken, tea-drinking woman who read poetry during her lunch break? After a moment of thought, he went after Angela. At first he could not find her. Then the failing light shone on a man with a cap pulled down low over his wide forehead and a wound on the back of his hand. Dan had seen the scar before because he'd stitched it up himself. Tank Guzman.

It was probably not outside the realm of possibility that Guzman was just coincidently attending the Beach Fest on the same night as Angela Gallagher, the woman who had watched his brother die. A chance meeting? And Lila just happened along, too?

Guzman stood in the shadows near a restaurant, the air rich with the scent of garlic and calamari, a cigarette in his fingers. Guzman wasn't interested in the food. He scanned the masses, a scowl on his face, until his gaze fastened on someone.

Angela?

Dan spotted her making a beeline for the parking lot. Several yards ahead of her was Lila, hastily edging her way through the throng.

Tank stubbed out the cigarette and tossed it to

the ground, following Angela. Dan closed the gap, intending to reach Angela before Tank did.

"Wait, Lila," he heard Angela call. "I need to talk to you about Tank. Please."

Lila wrenched open the door and got inside before slamming and locking it.

"Lila," Angela called again.

Time slowed down in Dan's mind. Lila's lips moved in some silent uttering as she turned the key. Her head turned the slightest bit, a frown on her brow as she watched Angela one moment longer. Her shoulder moved as she shifted into reverse.

"Lila," Angela cried one more time, coming within ten feet of the car.

Then there was a deafening bang and the smell of fire.

TWO

The blast took out the front right bumper and much of the engine compartment. It was the sound more than the force that caused Angela to stumble backward into the person behind her. Her head connected with the hard bone of a shoulder or chin. Tiny bits of glass pricked her face, and there was a vague sensation of heat. As she regained her balance, she caught a fleeting glimpse of Lila through the car window, pale profile wreathed in smoke.

Stunned, her legs turned to rubber. *Run, run, run*, her brain screamed. Her memory filled with the sound of rockets shrieking through the sky and the smell of burning diesel. A cry knifed the air. Was it her own? Lila's? A memory from the war?

Electricity surged through her limbs, overriding the fear.

The hood of the car was crawling with orange flames. The stink of burning plastic clogged her throat. Lila was still in the driver's seat, eyes closed, knocked unconscious by the explosion. Angela sprang forward but found herself caught. Dan Blackwater, gray eyes sparking, gripped her wrist.

"Stay back," he growled.

She yanked, almost ripping free of his grasp, but he was nearly six-four and strong. "She's got to get out."

He held her easily, moving her back several feet in spite of her resistance. "You can't help her right now." His tone was arrogant, reassuring, infuriating.

Can't help her? Unacceptable. She forced out a breath and stopped wriggling for a moment, just long enough for him to loosen his hold, and then broke away, running to the car and pulling on the door handle, which was hot to the touch. Locked. A crackle of flames burst from the engine compartment.

"Lila, wake up. Open the door," Angela screamed, trying the back door handle with no success. She pounded her palm against the glass as hard as she could.

Then Dan was on her again, grabbing her around the waist.

"Let me go," she shrieked. Was he just going to stay safely back and watch Lila burn to death or die of smoke inhalation?

Twisting from his grip she started hitting the glass again when he braced an arm around her and moved her back, lifting her off the ground.

"You're a coward," she yelled, flailing.

"That's enough," he roared.

She found herself tossed over his shoulder and carted away like a bag of laundry in spite of her screams. Blood rushed to her face as he hurried her away. A minute later, when he let her down, her head was spinning, cheeks hot.

He pushed her into the restraining hands of two twentysomething festivalgoers who had run to witness the aftermath of the explosion. "Hold on to her," he commanded. "Tightly." Each one grabbed an arm, and she was imprisoned.

"He's right, lady," said the one with the goatee. "There's nothing you can do."

Nothing? Should she stand by and watch while someone died right in front of her? Again? Her gaze traveled in horror to the car.

Free of her, Dan ran to the car, grabbing up a folding card chair the parking attendant had been using. Several people were already on their cell phones calling for help. Dan raised the chair and smashed it into the back window. The first blow did nothing. He raised the chair again, his muscled arms rigid with the effort, and slammed it into the glass. This time the glass gave, and the chair punched through.

"Man," said one of her captors. "That dude is strong."

Leaping onto the trunk, Dan kicked the rest of the glass in.

Another man, younger, wearing a Giants baseball cap, ran up waving a fire extinguisher. Without another word, he began spraying the powder against the flames coming from the front end of the vehicle.

She wasn't sure if Dan registered the second rescuer. Angela watched, pulse racing in terror, as he crawled through the back window.

"He's gonna be toast," said her captor. "Dude's gonna fry."

The fire extinguisher did little against the rising flames and the oily black smoke. She could hardly see the man in the cap, but the encouraging shouts of the onlookers meant he was still doing his best.

"Fire department's on its way," a lady shouted.

A minute ticked by, and she could see nothing through the smoke-shrouded windows. Had Dan decided to administer first aid right there in a burning car? Was he unable to get her seat belt unfastened? She swallowed. Had he been overcome by the smoke?

The driver's-side door was flung open with a groan of metal.

"He's unlocked it," she breathed.

A young couple raced up, took hold of Lila's shoulders and dragged her away from the flames. They laid her down gently on the pavement. Angela finally succeeded in breaking loose from her captors. She ran to Lila, dropping to her knees. To be sure she was still breathing, she held her cheek next to Lila's lips and felt the faint puff of air. Lila's pulse at her wrist was steady though faint. *Alive.* Angela stripped off her jacket and draped it over Lila's torso.

"We're going to get you to a hospital. Just hang on, Lila."

There was no response. Had she suffered a head trauma? Would she still be alive when they delivered her to the emergency room? There was such a minuscule distance between living and dead. Julio's crooked smile flashed through her mind. He'd smiled just before he'd died, smiled at her, the reason he had been cut down at the tender age of twenty. That smile would never leave her heart until her dying moment.

Angela wanted to pray aloud, but she found her mind whirling, a sickening cold enveloping her body. She clutched Lila's hand, squeezing, willing herself not to run away.

Shouts erupted all around her.

"Get out of there, man," someone yelled. "You're gonna burn alive."

It was several moments before she realized they were talking about Dan. The car was now enveloped in flames, black smoke filling the air. The driver's door stood open like a gaping mouth. No Dan. Several people tried to get closer, but the intensity of the heat drove them back.

Her face warmed at the nearness of the fire, but inside she remained cold. She wanted to help, but her legs would not move. *Then pray,* her heart begged. *Pray to God that the rescuer in the car will be delivered.*

But the prayer could not penetrate the surreal numbness. All she could do was watch.

Dan realized after Lila was pulled through the door to safety that he wasn't going to get out that way. The upholstered seats had begun to melt, and the flames licked up the steering column. He retreated the way he had come, over the front seat and into the back, just as the side window shattered. He dropped to the seat, covering his head from the cubes of safety glass that rocketed the width of the vehicle. His mind took him right back to Afghanistan, the moment when he had driven in the armored vehicle they affectionately nicknamed Nellie to assist a badly wounded soldier who could not be extracted from his Humvee quickly enough.

He remembered the rocket-propelled grenade that struck the road twenty feet from their transport, shaking the ground worse than any earthquake the California boy had ever experienced. A haze of dust, shouts of confusion, the intensity of the gunny who took charge and got his men to safety before they returned fire. Running boots, the punch of bullets into the ground, the groan of a shell-shocked man he finally realized was himself. The incredible courage he'd been honored to witness in the men and women he served, the realization that life was as delicate as a spring flower and as tenacious as a bulldog.

He'd learned not to try and shut out the memories, but to let them come, experience the pain again and extract himself from it. He did so now, as the glass settled all around him. Then he uncurled himself and continued on to the rear windshield, where there were helping hands, Good Samaritans braving the smoke, to assist him out and away.

Coughing, shaking the bits of glass from his hair, he saw that the ambulance had arrived and paramedics were working on Lila. A heavyset police officer had pushed the crowd back; another was talking into the radio and taking statements. He twisted around, blinking against the smoke that stung his eyes. Where was Angela?

A stocky cop approached, a smudge of black on his tanned face. "I'm Lieutenant Torrey. Do you need medical attention?"

"No. I'm looking for someone. There was a woman here, with Lila."

"Lila?"

"Lila Brown, the lady trapped in the car. I need to find the woman who was with her."

The kid with the goatee pointed toward the cliff. "She ran. That way. We tried to stop her, but she looked wild, you know?"

He thanked them. "I'll be back," he said to the cop.

The officer's thick brows drew together. "This

is a crime scene and I need to talk to you. I'll send an officer to find your friend."

"No," Dan said. "I'm going to find her now."

"I need you here." There was a warning in the tone.

He had no patience for questions. Not then. "My name is Dr. Daniel Blackwater. I live just up the beach. Here's my cell phone and wallet so you know I will return. I'll be back just as soon as I can." He strode away, feeling the officer's gaze burning into him, hearing a muttered oath behind him.

She looked wild, you know?

He did. He'd seen the seeds of that look when he'd not been able to save Julio Guzman, and he suspected her departure from Afghanistan had not been the end of it. In spite of some soreness along his belly from the glass that had cut through his shirt and into his skin, he moved through the crowd and jogged again to the beach.

The sun sank below the horizon just as he made it to the stairs, leaving him blinking to adjust to the meager light. The fog didn't help. Everything was gray shadows and glittering sea. He moved down to the sand, calling softly.

"Angela? It's Dan Blackwater."

The only answer was the waves scouring the shore. A distant boat motored by, heading to tie up at the nearby marina for the evening.

"Angela?" he said again.

He must have sensed her rather than noted any

sound. She sat, curled into a ball, knees drawn up under her chin, hands clasped together.

She didn't look up when he drew closer, so he stopped a few yards away and crouched down, making himself as small and nonthreatening as a six-four, soot-covered guy could be.

"Hey," he said.

She stiffened but did not look up. He could see only a glimpse of a tearstained face, hollow eyes that bored right into him down to a tender place he hadn't known was there. "Lila's on her way to the hospital, pulse is strong, looks like minor burns at this point. Breathing on her own. All good signs."

He heard a sniff. He moved closer until he could see the tight grip of her hands, the tension in her neck and shoulders, the slight trembling.

"The explosion was frightening," he said.

Sounds of crying. Slowly, very slowly, he touched her hand. "Hey. Why don't we talk? This stuff is hard, I know. It will help you to talk."

Her head jerked up then. "I don't need to talk. And you don't know anything about me."

He smiled. "Actually, I do. We were in the same place together, remember? A place that very few people in Cobalt Cove can conceive of, unless they served there, too."

She chewed her lip. "I don't want to talk about it."

"I didn't, either, but you've got to get help."

"I am the help," she snapped.

He got it then. "Oh. Because you're a chaplain, you're supposed to be the expert, the one who comforts others."

She didn't answer. When she looked out over the water, there was only despair on that lovely face, the look of someone who had been left behind, without hope of rescue.

"Angela," he started.

She waved a hand. "I'm sorry. The explosion and the fire. It got to me. It was silly to run. I'm sure the police want to talk to me."

"As a matter of fact, they do. I'll walk you back."

"Thank you, but I can find my way."

"Oh, they need to talk to me, too. I left at an inopportune moment." He gestured to the top of the stairs, where the silhouette of two approaching cops stood out against the dusky sky. "Torrey's steamed. Cops don't like it when you keep them waiting."

"Why did you then?"

"I wanted to find you."

She scrubbed the tears from her face with her sleeve. "No prize here."

He smiled. "I wouldn't be so sure." Offering a hand, he helped her stand. "Why did you come here to Cobalt Cove? Why were you talking to Lila?"

She hesitated. "I was looking for someone, and I heard Lila speaking to him on the phone."

"Who?"

There was a long pause. He guessed she was weighing whether or not to trust him.

"Tank Guzman," she said finally.

He raised an eyebrow. "Then I guess you accomplished your mission."

"What do you mean?"

"The guy who helped out with the fire extinguisher."

She stared at him.

"That was Tank Guzman."

THREE

Angela tried her best to focus on the questions being fired at her by Lieutenant Torrey. At Dan's insistence they had moved inside, to a table in the back room of the Grotto, a hole-in-the-wall seafood restaurant complete with a rowboat suspended on the wall and crab traps piled in the corner. The smell of cooking fish made her queasy.

"Why?" Torrey said again. She realized she hadn't heard the question.

"I'm sorry?"

"Why were you looking for Tank Guzman?" Dan supplied.

The lieutenant's wide chin went up. "Stay out of it, Dr. Blackwater."

Dan raised his chin. "This woman and I served together in Afghanistan. Lila Brown is my co-worker at the clinic. I want answers, too."

Angela knew Dan was close to being asked to step outside. For some reason, she wanted to avoid that. She took a deep breath. "Tank's twin brother was my chaplain's assistant in Afghanistan. I wanted to meet Tank."

Torrey's mouth twitched. "My son did some time there, too." He eased back in his chair, frame erect but a bit less stiff, brown eyes searching her face. "You're a navy chaplain and now a private investigator?" He'd taken a moment to do a quick search, she realized.

Angela blushed. "My family runs a PI firm. I help out. I have a few weeks of leave."

"Got a license?"

"No."

"You here to do some investigating on your own in Cobalt Cove? About Tank Guzman?"

She suddenly felt as if she was somehow under suspicion. *Stake your ground and hold on to it*, her marine father would have said. She sat up straighter. "No, I just wanted to find him and talk. I'd written him several letters over the past year, and he never replied until last week. He emailed me to arrange a meeting."

"Why now?" Torrey drummed thick fingers on the table. "Why would he want to meet you now? After blowing you off for so long? What's the urgency?"

"I don't know. From what I heard Lila saying on the phone, she was trying to discourage him from meeting with me. She came to the festival to beg him to call it off."

"That makes no sense."

"She said if he met with me, it might get them both killed."

"Are you sure he didn't tell you anything in the email that would explain why he wanted to meet you?"

She shook her head. He gave her an appraising look that went on long enough to make her uncomfortable. Police technique, she imagined.

There was another half hour of questioning, the last part of which was directed at Dan.

"How do you know Tank Guzman, Dr. Blackwater?"

Dan massaged his shoulder, grimacing. "I volunteer at the Cobalt Clinic. He came in maybe a month ago needing some stitches and a tooth repaired because he'd been in a fight, he said. Lila helped patch up his tooth, and I did the stitching."

"What was the fight about?"

Dan shrugged. "We just provide services to people who can't afford it. Period. We're not there to delve into their private lives unless they want to share."

"Convenient."

She saw Dan's mouth tighten a fraction.

"I didn't ask," he said, "and he didn't tell."

"Okay," Torrey said finally. "We'll take it from here." He got their contact numbers and leveled a look at Angela as he rose from the table. "Some advice. Tank Guzman is into some bad things. He's been in trouble, petty stuff, but he's not the kind of guy you want to get involved with. Best idea is to go back to Coronado and don't have anything further to do with Tank Guzman."

"Do you think he's dangerous?" she said.

Torrey's gaze drifted past her to the parking lot, where the blackened car still stood, waiting for the police to finish investigating.

"Go home, Ms. Gallagher. Leave the investigating to the cops."

Torrey left.

She realized Dan was staring at her.

"You're a private investigator?"

She smiled at the insanity of it. "Hard to believe a navy chaplain has a side job?"

He didn't return the smile. "No, but it's hard to believe that Guzman suddenly wanted to chat with a person he's avoided all this time." He pulled out his phone and typed something in.

"When did you send your last letter to Guzman?"

"It was an email. I sent it from my office account last month."

"How'd you find his email address?"

She raised her chin. "I work at a PI firm, remember? We find things out."

"Uh-huh." He read the tiny screen. "And when did your family decide to put up their website listing you as an associate of the firm like it says here?"

She swallowed. "Last month."

"So when you sent the email, he searched your name and it led him to Pacific Coast Investigations."

"Sounds right. Lila knew he'd contacted an investigator."

Dan pursed his lips. "Guzman's into some kind of trouble, or he wouldn't have run away after the fire."

"He might have been worried since he's got a past with the police, but he tried to help you rescue Lila—that has to show what he's made of."

"I'm just making an observation. Out of the blue, he asks you to come here, and then there's an explosion that nearly kills a woman and might have killed you if you were any closer," he added. "He takes off instead of talking to the police. That all seems a little strange to me."

Though she didn't say so, it seemed very strange to her, too. She felt suddenly bone weary and ready to drop. "I'm going to go to my hotel."

"I'll walk you back to your car."

An explosion that nearly kills a woman and might have killed you...

This time, she did not decline his offer.

Dan insisted on checking underneath Angela's car before she started it. There was no real reason to, except that his nerves were nagging him.

He gestured for her to roll down the window. "Where are you staying?"

"Blue Tide Inn."

"Can I get your cell number? In case I hear any updates about Lila?" He was suddenly uneasy that she might decline.

After a moment's pause she told him the number and then groaned. "My cell is in my jacket. I think it might have wound up going to the hospital with Lila. My car keys would have, too, if I hadn't put them in my back pocket."

"The hospital will keep it for you. I work there, or I did. I'm going to check on her tomorrow morning, anyway. I'll ask about it."

He felt her looking closer at him. "Don't you work there anymore?"

He rubbed his neck. "On leave, like you. Taking some time off. Injured my hand."

"Oh. The way you got Lila out of the car, I wouldn't have guessed it."

"A surgeon's hands have to be better than good. The tiniest slip and someone's dead." The words came out harsher than he'd meant. Something in her gaze made him uncomfortable, as if she saw things under the surface, things he didn't want anyone to see. "Anyway, I'll get the phone back for you."

"No need. I'll do it myself."

"Fair enough."

He stepped back so she could drive away.

She turned to him. "Do you need a ride?"

"No. My house is right up the beach."

She hesitated for another moment. "Dan, what I said before, about you being a coward. I'm sorry."

"No need to apologize."

"Yes, there is. You fought your way into a burning car to get Lila out. That's courage if I ever saw it."

He noted how the moonlight embedded sparks of light in her hair. "Oh, I don't know. For some folks, just facing another day requires more courage than I've got."

One more moment with her eyes locked onto his. Then she tucked her hair behind her ear and drove out of the parking lot. He watched until her car pulled out of sight. It was nearly nine o'clock. The crowds had dispersed, leaving only clusters of people sipping cups of coffee or walking down to the beach before heading home.

He took off at a slow jog, only two miles to his cottage. The term amused him. It was a dilapidated wood-sided claptrap, a far cry from the sleek five-bedroom house he'd owned before he'd gone to Afghanistan. He'd had visions of fixing the cottage up, restoring each warped beam and leaking faucet, but he hadn't and it didn't make much difference. The only thing that really mattered was the view from the sagging wraparound porch. The thundering of the Pacific beat a soothing rhythm day and night, steady, reassuring.

As he took the steps up to the porch, he said hello to Babs, the cat who had adopted him—or his porch, anyway. He spent a moment, as he always did, breathing in the grandeur of the ocean, which normally eased away all his troubles. God's work-manship. Incredible. That was one thing about his time in the desert. Somehow it made all the colors of the world brighter, more vibrant, upon his return.

Tonight, though, he found that his mind was not clear and easy. He liked Lila, appreciated her calm-ing way with patients and her gentle nature. If she was scared, he wanted to help. And then there was a certain navy chaplain. He flashed for a moment on her haunted green eyes, the deep green that re-minded him of new spring leaves. He could not rid himself of the feeling that Angela Gallagher was in trouble.

Angela wanted to call home and talk to her fam-ily, to reassure herself that all was well. After the disastrous last year, her youngest sister, Sarah, was still healing from the car crash that had taken their father's life. The killer who'd arranged it all would have murdered their sister Donna, as well, if God hadn't intervened and sent coast guard res-cue swimmer Brent Mitchell into their lives. Donna and Brent were enjoying their newlywed status, and her mother and sisters were busy tending to each other and the family business under the su-pervision of Marco, their longtime family friend. Maybe she could call Marco and tell him about all that had transpired, but he would be in a car speed-ing to Cobalt Cove in a matter of minutes, and she did not think she had the fortitude to handle a face-to-face with him.

She let herself into the small hotel room, decorated in soothing blues with a second-story balcony that looked over the front parking lot and out to the ocean beyond. She locked the door behind her, legs gone weak. Sinking down into a chair, she considered her options.

Go home, as Officer Torrey had suggested.

Stay and see if she could somehow locate Tank.

And then what? If he was a dangerous man, that plan would be just plain stupid.

"You're committed until tomorrow morning, anyway," she muttered to herself. There was no way she was going to leave Cobalt Cove without retrieving her cell phone and checking on Lila.

She wondered if she'd see Dan at the hospital. Her cheeks went hot as she considered what he must have thought after she'd bolted from the accident scene and hidden like a child on the beach. Yet his tone had not been condescending or pitying, the gray eyes gentle, or so she imagined.

With a sigh, she put the memory behind her and microwaved herself a cup of water, dunking in a tea bag before she opened the door to the balcony. The hotel phone rang and she answered it, gazing out at the sea, cradling the hot mug to her body with her free hand.

"Is this Angela Gallagher?"

"Yes. Who's calling?"

"You know who."

Her breath caught. "Tank?"

"Yeah. I need to talk to you."

Her nerves were rattled. "I don't think that's a good idea."

"I had nothing to do with that explosion."

"It's a police matter now."

"I need help. The way I see it, you owe me."

"How's that?"

"My brother died protecting you."

The words cut into her like bullet fragments. "I…I don't even know you."

"Doesn't matter. If my brother was alive, he'd have my back, but he's dead because of you."

The words robbed her of the power of speech. A throbbing pain filled her body.

"I need to talk to you now," he said. "Meet me at the diner across the street in fifteen minutes."

"I can't." She scrambled for an excuse. "I'm in my pajamas."

There was the sound of soft laughter. "No, you're not."

Terror balled in her stomach. Could he see her? She scanned the parking lot, quiet and dark. No, she told herself. He's bluffing. She let out a shaky breath.

"And you'd better drink your tea before it gets cold."

The phone slipped from her hand and fell to the floor, disconnecting the call.

FOUR

Dan was finishing up reading an article in a kayaking magazine when his cell phone rang. He turned down the music and answered. For a few seconds, there was no one on the other end, which sent the nerves cascading along his spine.

"Who's there?"

"Dan?" Another beat. "I'm sorry. I shouldn't have called."

He stiffened. "What's wrong, Angela?"

"Well…probably nothing."

"I was born nosey. Tell me."

"Tank called my room. I don't know how he got my number, but…"

He heard the catch in her breath. "What?"

"He's watching me. Maybe I should call the police."

"Yes, you should."

"But, I think he's in trouble. He—I…I want to talk to him."

Dan measured his words with care. "The police

would advise against it, and so do I." *Too arrogant?* He waited.

"I know, but I feel like I should."

"You think you owe him because of what happened to Julio." Overstepping for sure, but he couldn't take it back now.

No answer from her.

"You don't owe Tank anything. It's not smart to meet him."

"Thanks for the advice. Sorry to disturb you."

"You're going to do it anyway, aren't you?"

"I don't know. I'll think about it and decide."

Her tone was slightly miffed. He liked the hint of rebellion.

"I don't know why I called. I apologize. Good night."

"Hold on," he said. "As soon as you hang up, you're going to decide to go."

"Are you a mind reader now?"

"As a matter of fact, I am," he said in what he hoped was a jovial tone. "And your mind is saying it was a good idea to call that annoying Blackwater guy because he can help. I'll be there in five minutes. Don't leave your room until I get there."

"You're bossy."

He chuckled. "Only when I'm right," he said. "Stay put." Not waiting for her to rally an argument, he was out the door in moments. Normally he'd bike the two miles, but it was faster to take his Chevy. The truck rumbled over to the hotel.

Afraid she might have already left without him, he parked in the closest spot he could and jogged up to Angela's room.

"It's Dan," he said, knocking on the door, praying she hadn't gone on to meet Tank without him.

She opened the door wearing jeans and a thick sweater that matched her eyes. Her head cocked to the side, expression chagrined. "This is silly. I'm sure it's a misunderstanding."

He shrugged. "I'm up for silly. What else did he say to you?"

She relayed a few details about the call.

"All right. If it's a misunderstanding, we'll find out soon enough. Let's go to the diner."

"If he sees you with me, he might not come."

"We've met, remember? Over the hood of a burning car, so he probably knows I'm not a cop. If he's going to run, so be it."

She shook her head. "This cloak-and-dagger stuff is ludicrous."

"I thought you were a detective. Isn't that your stock in trade?"

A sliver of a smile lightened her face. There was a quick flash of a dimple, which thrilled and scared him. He'd always been a sucker for dimples until his gorgeously dimpled fiancée left him. *You deserved it, Dan. You came back from Afghanistan with different priorities. Wasn't AnnaLisa's fault. But still…dimples.*

"I'm only a detective on paper, remember?" she said, but she followed him out to the parking lot.

He strolled close and put an arm around her shoulders.

She stiffened but did not pull away. "What are you doing?"

"Just letting Tank know you've got backup, in case he wants to try anything."

"He wouldn't."

"There's a reason he isn't eager to take his problems to the cops. Let's play it safe until we know more."

The night was cold, and he felt her shiver. Then again, it might have been the insane day she'd had so far already. Explosions and clandestine meetings. She was right. Ludicrous, especially in the quiet town of Cobalt Cove.

The Beachbum Diner was an odd little spot, a throwback to the 1970s with booths upholstered in tan and yellow, with a menu as eclectic as the mismatched lighting fixtures.

Dan waved to Vin, the owner, and guided Angela to a corner booth. She slid in next to him, gaze darting around the place, which was fairly busy in spite of the late hour. Spillover festivalgoers devoured slices of pie and coffee, plates of waffles and eggs. No sign of Tank. "Can I get you something to eat?"

She jerked. "What?"

"Food." He waved at the owner. "Vin makes a mean stir-fry."

She raised an eyebrow and quirked her lips. "I was expecting burgers and omelets."

"He makes those, too. We should order something so we look less conspicuous. Besides, Vin is putting three kids through college. Sitters don't pay the tuition unless they're eating." Dan was about to go to the counter and order when Angela sat up straighter. She stared over his shoulder, lips pressed together as Tank joined them.

He sported a canvas jacket that had seen better days, turned up at the collar, and the same baseball cap he'd worn at the scene of the explosion. His face, though wider and dead serious, was indeed the image of his brother Julio's. Dan knew it was the face Angela saw in her memories, reliving the moments before Julio Guzman was shot. It was a face he'd never forget either, a patient lost in spite of every bit of medical expertise he could muster. Losing. He detested it.

Tank sat across from them, hunched low. "Why are you here?" he said to Dan.

"Waiting to eat. What do you want with Angela?"

"Didn't know you two were friends."

Dan let the comment sit there. The silence grew. Tank shifted, looking from one to the other and finally settling on Angela. "You really a detective?" he said, jutting his chin at her.

"My family owns a detective agency. I help out."

"Not a chaplain anymore?"

"I'm still a chaplain," she said quietly.

His eyes narrowed. "Get anybody killed lately?"

Dan heard Angela suck in a breath. He moved to toss Tank out of the booth, but Angela stopped him with a hand on his arm.

"Tank, there is no one sorrier than I am about what happened to your brother."

"Sorry doesn't matter. He's still dead. Except for my wife and my mother, he's practically the only family I had in this world, the only family I get to see, anyway."

Dan saw the delicate muscles of her throat tighten.

"People die in combat," Dan snapped.

"Yeah? Well, they're supposed to die for a reason, not to keep some preacher alive."

Dan leaned forward, jaw muscles twitching. "You're out of line, and you are not going to sit here and attack this lady. Am I making myself clear?"

"What do you know about it?"

"More about it than you ever will. I served in Afghanistan, too, kid."

"Soldier?"

"Doctor. And no one saw more death than we did, so keep a civil tongue in your head, smart aleck."

Tank's eyes went dark, hard as a stretch of bad road. For a moment, Dan wondered if the situation would escalate. He was ready if it did.

Tank slouched deeper into his jacket. "None of your business anyway, Doc."

"What do you want?" Angela said. "Why do you need a detective?"

"Because…" He tapped his fingers on the table, scanning the diners again. "Someone is going to kill me."

Angela wondered if she'd heard him right.

Dan raised an eyebrow. "Did you give them reason to want to do that?"

Angela shot Dan a look. "What he meant is, who would want to do that and why?"

"And why not go to the cops?" Dan put in.

"Listen," Tank said, hissing the word out. "I'm in trouble. I convinced Lila to help me, and you saw what happened to her. I need you to dig up some proof so I can take it to the cops so they'll believe me."

"Why won't they believe you now?" Angela said. "Especially if the person after you caused the explosion."

"I've had some trouble." He made a show of studying the green glass lamp hanging over their booth. "Done some drugs. And other things."

"Look, Tank," Dan said. "Let's hear it. Who's the mysterious villain gunning for you and why?"

"Not a mystery," Tank said, mouth in a tight line. "I know exactly who it is. I can show you a picture, for all the good it will do me, but he's smart and he knows how to get to me if I go to the cops. You need to help me," he said to Angela. "Prove he's into some bad stuff. Send him to jail."

His Adam's apple bobbed.

"I can talk to my partners," Angela said. "See what they think about taking the case."

"No." Tank slapped a hand on the table. "You need to do it. My brother said you were a stand-up lady, and he took three bullets keeping you alive—remember?"

Each word bored into her. Julio's smile drifted through her memory, even when he lay bleeding to death he had smiled at her. A stand-up lady? The woman who had insisted on going forward with the baptism that day, in spite of worsening threats?

"I will do everything I can to help you," she heard herself saying above the blood pounding in her veins.

"Angela…" Dan started.

Tank opened his mouth to speak, but in a moment he shot to his feet. Dan scrawled his cell number on a napkin and gave it to Tank. "We need to finish this conversation," Dan said, Tank pushed away from the booth, heading for the back exit.

"Wait," Angela said, starting after him.

Lieutenant Torrey's eyes narrowed as he came through the front door and scanned the patrons. He made his way over to Angela and Dan.

"Late night for you two. Figured you'd be asleep by now."

"I couldn't sleep," Angela said. She fired a "keep quiet" look at Dan. She wasn't sure what Tank had gotten himself into, but she could see the fear in his eyes, the spasming of his mouth when he'd spoken of his wife.

"Just came from the hospital. Looks like Lila is going to be okay. She's resting now; been given something to make her sleep. Going to interview her in the morning."

"Great news." Angela flicked a glance behind the lieutenant's shoulder to the window. She just made out Tank's blocky figure headed across the parking lot, head ducked low under his baseball cap.

She gestured for Torrey to sit, and he folded himself into the seat with a sigh. Vin approached the booth, holding a steaming cup of tea he offered to Torrey.

Torrey nodded his thanks. Vin retreated without a word. A stream of people left the restaurant, letting in a puff of cigarette-scented air. Torrey breathed deeply.

"Haven't had a smoke in eight years and, man, the smell still makes me pat my pockets looking for a cigarette."

"Addiction is powerful," Dan said.

"Yeah. That's what I was telling you about Tank. You were meeting him here, right?"

Angela wondered how he had figured that out. Though she'd decided to do her best to help Tank, she wasn't going to start lying to the police to do it. "We talked for a minute. He's scared someone is trying to kill him."

Torrey stayed still, but Angela had spent a career deciphering emotions. Torrey's face went curiously blank, his upper body stiffened so slightly she might have imagined it.

"Who?"

"He didn't get a chance to tell us."

Torrey wrapped a hand around the mug. "He gonna contact you again?"

"I don't know." Angela watched the steam from the tea drift upward. "I'll talk to him if he does, try and convince him again to go to the police." She paused. "But he doesn't seem to trust you."

"That's 'cause he's a criminal," Torrey said. "Most of 'em don't trust cops."

"Does he have a reason?" she asked softly.

His gaze locked on hers, eyes narrowing. "Maybe you should be careful about which side to pick here."

Dan cocked his head. "Lieutenant, that almost sounded like a threat."

Torrey drank a mouthful of tea. "No threat, just good advice." He pushed the tea away. "You know what Tank Guzman did before he came to Coronado?"

"No."

"He worked for a demolitions company."

Demolitions. The word kicked up the nerves along the back of her neck.

"Yeah," Torrey continued. "Demolitions. You know, the guys who knock down buildings?"

Angela nodded.

"Used to use those big wrecking balls but now, you know, things are high tech."

"High tech as in—" Dan started.

"Now they use explosives," Torrey finished. He got up. "Think carefully before you get into something you can't get out of." He flicked a card across the table at them. "Call me next time he arranges a meeting."

Torrey left. They sat in silence for a moment. Angela's mind spun. Whom to believe? Which one to trust? Before she would have followed her instincts, but now she didn't even trust herself not to bolt from the sound of a car backfiring. Several hours ago she'd been worrying that the man with the sport coat was stalking her. Paranoia. Fear. Whom to trust?

Dan reached out and took her hand. "Hey," he said softly. "Tell me what you're thinking."

His tone was so gentle, at odds with the raging torrent inside her. She realized she was clinging tightly to his fingers. Blushing, she let go.

"I'm going to call Marco at the office. He'll help me sort it out."

Dan sat back. She realized she'd been rude. "I appreciate your help, Dr. Blackwater."

"Dan."

"Dan. I'll call home." Saying it again made her

feel more sure. Though his eyes lingered on her face, she could not look at him without seeing him, exhausted, scrubs stained with blood, clinging to her hand as she collapsed to the hospital floor. He was the embodiment of a time she was trying without success to forget.

"Thank you again." She forced a smile, tone formal.

He gazed at her for another moment, before he got up and waited for her to slide out of the booth. "I'll walk you back to your hotel."

They strolled in silence, and this time he did not put his arm around her. It was better that way. Since Afghanistan, she found she did not like to be touched, not even by her family. She found her key card and slid it into the lock. He held the door for her as she entered, reaching to take his phone out of his pocket.

"Got a text." He looked closer. "It's from Tank. The message is, 'This is the guy who's gonna kill me.'" He frowned and held the screen for her to see.

She took it from him, stared at the picture. Her body went suddenly cold.

"You know him?"

"Oh, yes," she said in a whisper. "I know him."

Dan saw her bite her lip so hard he was sure it would bleed. Her body went stone stiff, as if she would crack if he touched her.

He put a hand on her shoulder. For a moment,

they did nothing but breathe. Sometimes, he thought, that was enough. Then she cleared her throat.

"I saw him for the first time this morning." She told him about her fall and how he'd offered help, retrieved the contents of her purse. "I thought he was too interested, but I chalked it up to paranoia." A flush of color painted her cheeks. "I've been unsure... It's a hard adjustment, coming home, you know?"

"I do."

"He knew my name." She stared at the picture. "I'm beginning to think he knew my identity before I dropped my purse. Who is he?"

"His name is Harry Gruber. He owns a trucking company."

Angela cocked her head. "You know him?"

"Sure do. Gruber is a respected guy in this town. Actually, his donations fund the clinic where I volunteer."

"Is he a friend?"

"Acquaintance," Dan said. "We've done some charity events together, fun kid days at the clinic and such."

"So why would a man like that have any interest in killing Tank Guzman?"

"Could be Tank is completely wrong. His integrity is still in doubt." He shook his head. "What is Lieutenant Torrey going to have to say about this development?"

She sighed. "I'll call the office. They're better at this than I am." The dim light shadowed her face, adding to the fatigue.

"It can wait until tomorrow." He flipped on the rest of the lights and made sure the sliding glass door was secure, the curtains drawn.

As he turned to go there was a wondrous smile on her face. It stopped him in his progress to the door.

She caught his surprise. "I was just thinking that my gut told me Harry Gruber was up to something. Maybe my instincts do work, at least a little." She sighed. "Something works, even if it's just a small thing."

She looked so delicate standing there, her slender silhouette framed by the lamplight, arms wrapped around her waist as if offering herself a hug. He wanted to do the same.

"It's not a small thing. That's a little window into yourself," he found himself saying. "God's telling you you're still in there—you aren't lost. I had those little windows, too, after I came back. We can talk about it, if you want to."

She looked away, cheeks flushed, and he knew he'd overstepped. "Thanks. I appreciate that."

It was a dismissal, and there was nothing he could do to erase the distance between them. *Pushy, Blackwater, as usual.* "Okay. Call me if you need anything. Good night, Angela."

"Thank you," she said, "for your help."

Had he helped? He considered as he returned to the truck, ruefully plucking the ticket he'd received off the windshield for parking in a red zone. In his haste to get to Angela after Tank's call, he had parked in the first spot he'd found. The ticket had been issued by Lieutenant Torrey.

Tank's accusation of Harry Gruber wasn't going to sit well with Torrey. Angela's guilt would make her take Tank's side even if the kid was flat-out lying. She'd made enemies on both sides.

Why did it prey on his mind as he drove home?

Because you're nosy and you always want to manage people's lives whether they want you to or not.

All true.

Yet he felt something other than nosiness as he stood out on the deck, watching the ocean crawl by, waiting for a sleepiness that would not come.

FIVE

Six o'clock could not arrive quickly enough. Angela had slept no more than a few hours, finally getting up before sunrise to shower and make a pot of instant coffee, most of which was already gone. At the stroke of six, she dialed, knowing that Marco would be in the office after his early morning workout at the local gym. Marco's routine was as predictable as the sunrise.

She also knew he would not answer the phone unless there was a very good reason. The man despised technology.

"Marco," she said into the machine after the beep. "It's Angela. There's been some trouble."

"What trouble?" he said as he picked up the phone. She heard noise in the background.

"Is Candace there this early? What's wrong?"

"Nothing," Candace called from the background. "I was picking Donna and Brent up from the airport."

Angela smiled. "How was their honeymoon?"

"Just a minute," Marco muttered. "Gonna try and put this thing on speakerphone." There was the sound of Marco pressing buttons, and then they were disconnected. She smiled, picturing him there, big fingers stabbing away at a phone that was beyond his comprehension, brilliant though he was. She was about to redial when there was a knock at the door.

Her breath caught. Too early for housekeeping. Skin prickled on the back of her neck, the way it had when she'd realized Tank was watching her in her hotel room. Enemy or friend? Unsure, she crept to the door. There was no peephole. She placed a hand on the door as if she could somehow feel who it was through the panel.

"Who is it?" she called.

"Dan Blackwater."

Relief and tension rippled together through her insides. She thought their connection was over; she was hoping, anyway. He was the past for her, the cruel, savage past that would not seem to get out of her present. The seconds ticked on as she tried to think of a polite way to get him to leave.

"Hey, not to be pushy, Angela, but this coffee is burning my hand. I forgot to get those cardboard sleeve thingys."

She yanked open the door. He held two to-go cups, a white paper bag tucked under his arm. "What are you doing here?"

"I will excuse that ungracious tone if you'll

please take this coffee." He thrust the cup at her, and she took it. "I figured you could use some breakfast. I'm on my way to the hospital. Thought we might as well go together, since we both have some questions for Lila."

Her computer beeped, saving her from trying to rally a polite refusal. "Hold on—that's Marco. He's trying to Skype this time. Candace must be helping him."

She opened up Skype, and Marco's shaved head filled up the screen, Candace peering over his shoulder.

"What trouble?" Marco demanded.

She filled him in and introduced Dan. "He's, um, I knew him in Afghanistan."

Marco was silent for a moment. A retired navy man, he understood the significance of that statement. "Okay. I'm leaving now for Cobalt Cove. I'll see which one of your sisters is available to come with me. Don't meet with Tank or Gruber until I get there."

Candace blew out a breath. "I'd come, too, but Tracy is in a school play, and they've got practice every day."

Angela smiled, thinking of her sweet six-year-old niece. Tragic that the child had lost her father in Iraq when she was barely old enough to know him. Then to lose her grandfather a month ago. Angela swallowed the hard lump in her throat. "Did she land the coveted role?"

"Yep, she's the snowflake in the winter play. There will be sparkles and white tights and a tiara."

Angela laughed. "Can't wait to see it."

"Sarah and I will look into things on this end."

"How is she?"

Candace frowned in a way that told Angela everything. Sarah had been at the wheel when their father's car was forced off the road and he was killed. Her emotional trauma far outweighed the physical damage from the crash. "Still not sleeping, and Mom and I have to practically force food down her throat."

"I'll be back soon and…" Angela trailed off. How could she comfort her sister when she couldn't even help herself? She regrouped and straightened her shoulders, hoping Dan hadn't noticed the lapse.

When they ended the call, Dan offered to drive her to the hospital.

"No need. I'll drive myself. I have some things to do afterward." At the moment she had precisely nothing to do until Marco arrived, but she didn't want to be in the car next to Dan. His silver gaze searched her face as if he understood completely that she was avoiding him.

She thanked him again for the coffee and took the scone he offered before they got into their vehicles and drove to the hospital. Lila Brown was being treated on the fifth floor.

The hallway was quiet. A nurse returned Angela's cell phone and pointed them to room 504.

The smell of the hospital assaulted her, the odor of disinfectant and, she imagined, despair. So many stories ended at such places; she felt as if her own story had ended in a hospital, too, far away on foreign soil.

She sensed Dan looking at her.

"I guess you spend a lot of time in hospitals, for your chaplain work."

She had. But now she practically had to force herself through the doors, her visits to patients strained, requiring her to seclude herself afterward just to get her rampaging emotions under control. Her commanding officer had asked her to take a month off. Humiliating but she had complied meekly.

"You, too," she managed. "When are you going back to surgery?"

His gaze drifted away. Surprising. He was tall, strong, self-assured to the point of arrogant, but something uncertain crept over his face, a shadow she didn't understand.

"Not sure," he said. "Lila's room is right over there."

As they rounded the corner, there was a crash, the sound of metal hitting the tile floor. Dan sprinted ahead, and, after a second of paralysis, Angela followed. They burst into the room.

A nurse looked up, startled. She held a roll of gauze in one hand. A vase of flowers had been upended, the white roses lying in a puddle of water on the floor. The bed sheets were tousled.

"What happened?" Dan demanded.

"She freaked out."

"Lila Brown?'

The woman nodded. "She was asleep. I needed to change her dressing. I woke her. Tried to cheer her up by showing her the flowers. She opened the card and screamed. Grabbed her clothes and ran. Moved so fast I gouged her with the scissors. What's wrong with that girl?"

"Which way did she go?"

The nurse shrugged. "Dunno."

Dan charged out into the hallway.

"I'll go call security," the nurse said as she left.

Angela was about to follow, when she spotted the tiny white envelope lying half under the bed, the little card next to it.

There was no message on the card.

Blank.

A cold knot formed inside her.

She picked up the envelope. It was empty, she thought at first.

Feeling a subtle bump through the glossy paper, she looked inside.

A snippet of dark hair, fine and silky.

Like a child's hair, she thought.

A child.

She dropped the envelope and bolted out the door.

* * *

Dan wasn't sure which direction Lila had headed, but he knew he had to get to her. He ran to the nearest elevator and pressed the button. The light indicated it was on the way down. *Lila?*

He sprinted for the stairs and raced down to the fourth floor. He was going to keep running, figuring she was headed for the ground floor exit, when he noticed the stairwell door that opened out onto the fourth floor was not completely closed; a white sock on the floor kept it from latching. Bursting through the door, which creaked open with a squeal, he caught the attention of a short, dark-haired woman.

It was Patricia Lane, a surgeon at the hospital. "Patricia?"

"Dr. Blackwater?" The woman goggled. "What are you doing? Is something wrong?"

"I'm looking for a girl who just ran out of her room. I thought maybe she came up here."

She clicked her pen closed. "I've been checking the charts for the past fifteen minutes and I haven't seen anyone running through except for you."

He saw no sign of Lila anywhere, just the normal hustle and bustle. An older bearded man appeared at the doorway to his room. He scratched his close-cut beard.

"Can I get some food? I'm hungry." He rubbed a sleeve under his nose.

The man looked vaguely familiar. Dr. Lane hastened to his side. "Please sit down. I'll have the nurse bring you something right away."

The man returned to his room, muttering to himself.

Dr. Lane smiled. "Sometimes we get a wanderer. You know what that's like."

"I do."

But his mind was only on one patient. Lila Brown. He walked the length of the floor and found no sign of her. Perhaps the sock had been a ruse?

Dr. Lane was staring at him. "I told you. She didn't come here. Don't you believe me?"

"Of course." He returned to the stairwell door, mulling it over. The sock was protruding through to the inside, which meant Lila had arrived on the fourth floor and exited back out to the stairs. Could it have been dropped by another visitor or patient? Not likely. Patricia Lane was a stern taskmaster. The nurses and orderlies he'd worked with at the hospital were top-notch, as well.

He walked Patricia to the door and pointed out the sock.

"Strange," she said. "I can't imagine how that got there."

"I'm sure it was Lila," Dan said. "She opened the door and dropped the sock. She must have gone back out again if you didn't see her. Is it possible you were engrossed in your work and you missed her?"

Patricia's lips thinned into a tight line. "I would

have noticed. I'm not oblivious to what goes on in my own hospital."

"I wouldn't even suggest that."

Her face was stony, eyes hard and unblinking. "I'm glad to hear it."

"There must be another explanation," he said. "Leave the sock there and I'll get the police on it."

"Fine. I'll continue my rounds." She turned and strode away.

Dan mentally ran through the scenario. Patricia Lane was an excellent doctor with a stellar reputation. She must have been focused on her work and not heard the stairwell door open.

It was the most likely answer. But if she'd been standing at the desk checking charts not five feet from the stairwell door, how could she not have heard it open?

But what reason could Dr. Lane have for lying?

A sudden chill crept down his spine. Careful not to disturb the sock, he headed downstairs to find Angela.

Angela emerged into the hallway, and a nurse pointed out the direction Dan had taken to the stairs. Angela hurried to the stairwell door. One of them would surely intercept Lila. She intended to ask on each floor as she went if anyone had seen the girl.

She started the plunge down the steps. Her feet echoed oddly in the space. Her chest tightened up as the walls closed in around her in an ugly cement fist.

Keep going. Don't let the thoughts catch up with you.

Racing down, she was about to exit on the fourth floor, but she heard a murmur of voices from farther down the stairwell. She continued onto the third floor and listened. No further noise. Her imagination?

Pressing on, she found a hospital gown tossed onto the cement. It was still warm to the touch. Lila had taken a few frantic moments to change clothes.

She's getting out of here for sure. What had scared her so badly that she'd bolt without even taking the time to dress properly? Tension coiled in her gut now like a live serpent, and she continued racing down. Almost to the second floor, she was startled when she heard the door below her open.

"Lila," she called out. "Wait. Don't leave." Now she was taking the steps two at a time, clutching the railing to keep from falling.

Six steps down, a man came into view, standing at the bottom landing, just in front of the exit door.

Harry Gruber.

He smiled.

Her breath caught, heart thundering.

She squashed the surge of panic. *You're not trapped.* She could run up and escape through the second-floor door. *Stay calm. You're in control.* Her nerves raced as if they had not gotten the message.

"Odd us meeting again," Gruber said.

She swallowed. *Take charge of the situation.* "Yes, it is, Mr. Gruber."

If he was surprised that he'd learned her name, he didn't show it. "Especially here." His lips curved in disgust as he gestured. "I hate hospitals, don't you? Only come when I don't have any other choice. All those desperate people, hoping to be cured and wondering how they'll pay for all the pills and procedures. Patients paying for the green fees for the fat-cat doctors. That's why I started up my clinic."

He wore khakis and a short-sleeved shirt neatly buttoned, plaid against a pale yellow background. "What are you doing in the stairwell?"

He raised an eyebrow. "I could ask you the same thing."

The air in the stairwell closed in, her palms went damp, breathing shallow, the familiar sense that her body was about to spin out of control. *Don't give in.* She'd decided to go back up, outrun him to the next floor, when she saw a man step out onto the landing above her. Someone to help. She let out a gasping breath.

He looked over the railing at her, unsmiling, black eyes scanning.

"Sir…" she started, moving toward him. Something in the flat expression on his face made her pause. He was a blurred image of Harry, a relative, a brother. He rested his palms on the railing and stared at her.

Something cold slithered up her back. Cut off. No escape. She forced herself to keep breathing and speak calmly. "Is that a friend of yours?"

"My brother, Peter."

She looked again at Peter, still as granite and just as cold.

Terror ricocheted inside her. *Keep talking. Stall until Dan comes. Or another passerby.* "Did you see a woman run by here?" she asked Harry.

"A woman?" He laughed. "Women run by me all the time and never even look back." He pushed open the door and held it for her. "Were you going to exit? Allow me."

The sunshine flooded through the door, enticing her with the promise of escape. She considered running back up to the second floor and trying to pass Peter, but the exit door was open wide, fresh air only a few feet away. Tantalizing. More than anything else, she desperately wanted to run toward freedom, away from Harry and his brother.

Keeping out of reach, she edged closer, ready to scream for help if Gruber made any move to detain her. He didn't.

Had she imagined a threat where there wasn't one?

Sweat dampened her brow. Paranoia? Were Harry Gruber and his brother just two innocent bystanders? Neither one had touched her or uttered so much as a single threat. Doubt flooded in.

As she passed, she noticed something that didn't belong.

There, against the background of Harry's neat yellow shirt, was an imprint left by two bloody fingers pressed against his chest.

SIX

Dan had just checked the third floor and entered the stairwell when he heard Angela's scream. A full-out gallop down the steps brought him to the bottom in moments. He slammed through and found Angela bent over, sucking in deep breaths in the empty parking lot.

He grabbed her by the shoulders, heart pounding. "Are you hurt?"

She stared at him, mute with terror. No visible signs of injury. He gripped her hands. "Purse your lips like you're blowing out a candle and breathe like that."

She did, and the hyperventilation began to dissipate. After a few moments, she was able to straighten, still clutching his fingers in hers.

"What happened?"

He saw her throat convulse as she swallowed. "Harry Gruber and his brother were in the stairwell." She told him about the bloody print on

Harry's shirt. "You must have passed them when you came down."

"There was no one there. Just a hospital gown left on the steps."

She gaped, letting go of him. "I just ran by them. They have to be there. Harry and his brother, Peter."

"I passed no one, Angela," he said gently.

"Are you saying I'm making this up? That I'm hallucinating or something?" The beginnings of angry tears shone in her eyes.

"Not at all," he said calmly. "They must have returned to the second floor. Probably took the elevator down to the lobby and left."

A stroke of calm trickled across her face. "So… you believe me?"

He searched her face for a moment, wishing he could see the tiniest flicker of confidence there. Instead he noted only a desperate need for reassurance. "Yes, I believe you. Something weird is going on at this hospital."

A little flicker of emotion told her he'd eased her turmoil, at least for a moment. He told her about the sock.

"What is happening in this town?" Angela said.

"I don't know. I asked a nurse to call the police." He scanned the parking lot. "Where did Lila go?"

"I'm not sure, but I think I know why she ran. Does Lila have a child?"

"She mentioned a son once."

"I think someone left a lock of his hair along with the flowers," she said, face pale. "As a message."

A tight band fastened itself around his chest. Threats to Lila's child? Things were growing darker every moment, like a shadow gradually blotting out the sun. "We have to find her. Now. I'm going to drive the nearby streets. Can you...?" He tried for tact. "Do you want to sit down in the lobby and wait for me?"

Her chin went up, a flame kindling in her green eyes. "I can make it to your truck."

He thought how magnificent she looked. Strong and scared, undefeated even in her terror. Strengthened by God, even if she didn't feel it. They made it to his truck and checked out all the side streets adjacent to the hospital. No sign of Lila. By the time they made it back to the hospital, Lieutenant Torrey was already there.

He jutted his chin at them. "Talked to the nurse. Lila bolted, huh?"

Dan and Angela filled him in on the hair and the dropped sock, on Harry Gruber's appearance in the stairwell and his bloodstained shirt.

Torrey's eyebrows raised a notch higher with each revelation.

"So you're accusing Gruber of what, exactly?" Torrey said.

"Not accusing him of anything. Just telling you the facts," Dan said. "He can try and explain the bloody shirt."

He flicked a glance over Dan's shoulder. "I guess he can, since he's standing right over there."

Angela jerked around. He turned to find Harry Gruber striding over, an affable smile on his face, a khaki jacket zipped to his chest.

"Is there a problem, Max?" Gruber said.

Max. The two were tight.

Lieutenant Torrey did not return the smile. "Seems we've had a patient fly the coop. Ms. Gallagher says you had contact with the woman as she fled. Lila Brown. Did you and your brother encounter her in the stairwell a half hour ago?"

"Me?" He laughed. "I've been waiting to visit Lila. The doctor was in with her when I arrived. Always waiting in these hospitals. Doctors don't value anyone's time but their own." He flicked a look at Dan. "Haven't been near the stairwell. My brother is at the clinic. I just called him. It's been crazy busy, but we're going to try and squeeze in a little fishing time. There's a perch with my name on it out there—I can feel it." He held out his cell phone. "Call him if you'd like."

"You're lying," Angela said.

A hurt expression crossed his face. "Hey, now. I don't know how we got off on the wrong foot, since I hardly know you, but calling me a liar?"

"Take off your jacket," Angela commanded. "There was blood on your shirt. Lila's blood. You can't lie about that."

Harry frowned, flicking a glance at Torrey. "I'm just a truck driver, but I'm fairly certain I don't have to comply. Do I?"

Torrey shifted. "Maybe not technically, but what's it going to hurt, taking off your jacket?"

"Unless I have something to hide," Gruber finished, eyes hard as wet stones.

"No offense intended."

"Well, I am offended," Gruber said. "Wouldn't you be?"

Dan stared down at the shorter man. "Like he said, what's it going to hurt, Mr. Gruber? Put the whole situation to rest right here." There was a challenge in his tone, and Gruber did not miss it.

"We've always been colleagues, I thought. You work at my clinic, Dan, and this is as far as your loyalty goes?"

"Your clinic does good work for many people, and I am pleased to be a part of that. This is a different issue."

"You're not pleased," Harry hissed. "It strokes your ego, working with the down-and-out. The brilliant surgeon walks among the lowly masses, doling out free care for which you charge exorbitant prices in your hospital setting. Feeds your God complex, doesn't it?"

Dan refused the bait. "Open your jacket, unless you've got some reason to refuse to comply."

"Refuse to comply," Gruber said, shaking his

head. Anger coiled in his voice. "Lofty words. I guess I never really saw you clearly before, Dr. Blackwater."

I guess I made the same mistake, Dan thought. He'd taken Gruber at face value, a genial guy, generous, a philanthropist, a salt-of-the-earth type who loved tacos and fishing trips.

"On his shirt," Angela insisted, "there are bloody fingerprints where Lila must have touched him. He took her, maybe abducted her."

Harry waved a hand. "Hang on just a minute. Before I am accused of everything since the Hindenburg explosion, let me clear my name." He yanked down the zipper of his jacket.

Angela's expression went slack with shock.

Instead of a yellow shirt, Gruber now wore a tee with "Gruber and Gruber Trucking" emblazoned on the front.

The shirt was a blinding white, clean as a rainwashed beach.

There was no way what Angela was seeing could be true. Her reeling mind could hardly take it in. "He changed shirts."

Gruber sighed. "Think what you want. Look, Lieutenant Torrey, I hope Lila is all right. She's a great employee, the patients at the clinic love her and my brother, Peter, thinks she's the bee's knees. If she's in trouble, I'll help you and her any way I can, but I didn't see her in the stairwell. And this lady—" he shot a disdainful look at Angela "—is obviously too distraught to be of much help."

"The lock of hair," Angela said, wishing she had taken it from Lila's room. "In the florist's card. That proves that someone was trying to scare Lila by threatening her son."

Gruber arched an eyebrow. "And I suppose that's to be laid at my doorstep, too? I've been nothing but kind to Lila, helping her finish dental hygiene school so she could support the kid. She'll tell you the same thing once you find her." He chuckled. "Besides, I really don't have the time to be a criminal mastermind. I've got a trucking company to run and two grandkids to spoil."

"Mr. Gruber, I am sorry to have bothered you," Torrey said. "I'll contact you if we have further questions."

Gruber nodded and strode away, whistling.

"He's lying," Angela insisted.

Torrey rubbed a hand over his fleshy cheeks. "Right now I have nothing that proves anything happened other than Lila decided to check herself out. You two need to come with me to Lila's room and we'll see about this card you say you found."

You say you found. Torrey thought she was lying. Or crazy.

Was she? Or was Torrey involved in whatever had just happened? He was on a first-name basis with Gruber. Her palms grew cold and sweaty as they headed to the elevator. As they passed each floor she worked on breathing, trying to calm her rattling nerves. Dan's arm slid around her.

She wanted to push away, but she desperately needed that grounding touch. She shot a look at him.

He winked. A silly gesture that reassured her more than a volume of words. He believed her. He knew she was not crazy. Dan Blackwater was standing with her. She was not alone, at least in this.

They found the orderly with a broom and dustpan, sweeping up the shattered remains of the vase and fallen roses.

Angela edged past Torrey. "It should be here on the floor." She searched. Nothing. Dropping to hands and knees she checked under the bed and in the broken glass in the dustpan.

"Where is it?" she asked the orderly.

"What?"

"The envelope that came with the flowers."

He shrugged. "I don't know. I just got here."

He was tall, a good six feet, whip thin with a face pockmarked by acne.

"Are you sure you didn't see it?" she asked.

His tone grew surly. "Are you saying I'm lying?"

"She's just asking a question," Dan said.

"I do what I'm told," he said. "They tell me to clean, I clean. No one told me to make an envelope disappear."

His smock was loose fitting, covering baggy

pants that no doubt had pockets. She had no reason to accuse him or suspect him even. She stepped back and allowed him to finish sweeping up.

Torrey called for the nurse, who said she'd never seen any envelope, but she had been distracted by Lila's violent bolt from the room. The woman appeared bewildered by the whole affair.

They continued upstairs. Dan took them to where he'd seen the sock.

His mouth opened in surprise. She crowded in close behind him to look. There was nothing there, no sign of the sock.

They approached Dr. Lane, who emerged from an exam room, scribbling on a chart. She looked at them over the top of her glasses, gaze lingering for a moment on Lieutenant Torrey. "Another problem?"

"The sock is gone," Dan said, gesturing to the stairwell.

She stared at him. "I told the floor staff to leave it, per your orders. We've been using the other stairwell when necessary."

"Well, it's gone now," Dan said.

Dr. Lane summoned the shift nurses and custodian. No one claimed responsibility for removing the sock.

"I apologize for the confusion," Dr. Lane said to Torrey. "There was a sock there," she told him, "just as Dr. Blackwater said, but I can't tell you what happened to it. I'm sorry."

"Thank you for your time, Dr. Lane," Torrey said.

Lane excused herself, and, as she passed, Angela noticed that her forehead was damp with sweat. Was it warm in the hallway? Angela's hands were still ice-cold from her earlier encounter with Gruber so she could not accurately tell. Again her mind swiveled between suspicion and fear that she was becoming paranoid.

Once they were alone, Torrey folded his arms across his barrel chest. "No sock, no envelope, no bloody fingerprints, no witnesses to corroborate Gruber or his brother being in the stairwell."

"Gruber did something to Lila Brown," Angela insisted through gritted teeth. "And he's lying about everything. His brother's involved, too."

"Nice story. Look, I don't know what game you're playing here, but you are the stranger in Cobalt Cove." His cheeks took on a reddish flush. "You arrive in town and accuse a longtime resident of harassing a woman with no shred of proof to your claims."

Dan moved forward. "Lila's in danger. Her car blew up. That's got to be enough proof of danger for you."

"We're investigating that, if you recall, Doctor."

"You should look for Lila," Dan told him.

"Don't tell me how to do my job," he snapped, chin thrust out. "We will look for Lila, but as of this moment, there is no proof that a crime has been committed in this hospital. Stay out of this investigation, and stay away from Harry Gruber."

He turned on his heel and marched out.

Angela finally allowed herself to be led back to Dan's truck.

"Gruber snatched her—he must have," she murmured. "Maybe the orderly or the nurse took the envelope and the sock. They might be helping Gruber."

"There's still the big 'why' here. Why would Gruber go after his employee?" Dan stared out the windshield without turning the key. "And how would he have forced her into a car or his trunk without anyone seeing? Lila was scared, but able-bodied enough to run down four flights of stairs. She would have fought."

"His brother was there. Two men against one woman."

"Maybe." He drummed his fingers on the steering wheel. "Maybe she got by him."

Angela chewed her lip. "Dr. Lane and Lieutenant Torrey. I got the oddest sense that they know each other."

"Probably. They've both lived in Cobalt Cove for a long time."

"What type of surgeon is Dr. Lane?"

"Started as a urologist in her early days. Now she's a kidney transplant specialist. There were times when our paths crossed." His voice faded away.

"When?"

"If a patient didn't survive, if they were an organ donor, she consulted."

She looked into his gray eyes, which had darkened to a pewter, and knew he was in the grip of memories, bad ones. "That must be hard, to lose a patient."

He blinked. "I remember every one I lost in peacetime. Some were harder than others, but none of it could compare to what happened in Kandahar."

And then she was holding his hand, squeezing to show what she could not say. Before she would have prayed; now she could only listen. *I know you lost so many in Afghanistan. Too many. I'm sorry. So sorry.*

As if he read her mind, he answered, "In Kandahar, there was a constant flow of wounded. Often I saw soldiers on the worst days of their lives. The last day they would walk, the final moment they would see, the beginning of a tortuous road. Those were bad, but the others..." He swallowed. "The ones that didn't make it, the ones I couldn't save. I knew they were with God, but their family's pain, their worst nightmares, were just beginning."

She knew. Her pain, her worst nightmare, began when Julio had died in her place. Tears crowded her eyes. It was probably only a few moments, but it seemed like a very long time they sat there in his truck, side by side holding hands, allowing grief and memory to swirl between them like the steel-blue waters of Monterey Bay. When it became too much, the pain too strong for her to endure, she pulled away.

Realizing her face was wet with tears, she patted her pockets and located a tissue. "It's only ten-thirty," she said, checking her watch, steering them back onto safe ground. "My family won't be here until tonight. I guess I should go back to the hotel and try to do some research."

"Or we could go find Tank."

She blinked. "How? We don't know where to look."

"I went to the clinic this morning and pulled his file. I know his address."

Her mouth fell open. "And what were you going to do with that info?"

"Find him. Talk to him. Tell him I'd help him so he wouldn't involve you in trouble."

She glared at him. "You shouldn't be doing things on my behalf and especially not without my knowledge."

He regarded her with a maddeningly calm expression. "Okay. I'm going to talk to Tank. Now you have knowledge. Do you want to come or not?"

"But Lieutenant Torrey told us to keep out of the investigation—"

"Tank is a former patient. I have a right to check on him. Besides, I'm perfectly comfortable disobeying orders when necessary."

She could not repress a smile at the outright cockiness. "You're arrogant—you know that?"

"So I've been told."

"By whom?"

"Plenty of people, but notably my former fiancée, AnnaLisa."

"Did she also mention that you're bossy?"

"Repeatedly. Bossy, freakishly neat, overly competitive and a sore loser with a limited fashion sense." He grinned. "Now that we've got that established, are you in or out on the Tank visit?"

Angela thought that Dan Blackwater just might be one of the most infuriating and completely charming men she had ever met. "I'm in," Angela said, buckling her seat belt. "Let's go."

SEVEN

They drove to the tiny rented house on the edge of Cobalt Cove, almost at the town limit. The street was lined with parked cars and old pines that dumped needles in clumps on the cracked side-walks.

"Tank's place is one-twenty-seven." Dan pulled the truck to the curb, next to a one-story stucco house with barred windows and a wild scalp of lawn. An elderly lady walked past leading two tiny dogs, eyeing them carefully as she did so.

"Neighborhood watch?" Dan said.

Join the parade, Angela thought. Why did it feel as if everyone was watching them? Shaking off the ripple of anxiety, she got out and headed for the front door. She rapped on the metal, the sound echoing.

A dog barked in the neighbor's yard, wet nose visible through a knothole in the warped wood. Angela knocked again. "It's Navy Chaplain Angela Gallagher," she called. "I'm a friend of Tank's, Mrs. Guzman. Please open the door."

She leaned close. "I think I heard someone," she whispered to Dan. Seconds ticked by.

"Please, Mrs. Guzman," she tried again. "Tank's in trouble and we want to help."

The door opened a crack, grating against the fastened security chain. A young woman with wavy dark hair peered out, frowning. "What do you want?"

"We need to talk to Tank," Angela said. "Are you Mrs. Guzman?"

"My husband is not home."

"Where is he?" Dan said.

Her eyes grew more fearful. "Who are you?"

"This is Dr. Blackwater. He's a surgeon. He treated Tank at the clinic."

Dan peered down at her, bending a little. "Tank spoke of you, Mrs. Guzman. Your first name is Cora, right?" Dan offered a smile that even Angela had to admit was charming. "Tank told me you were going to scold him solidly for fighting in the bar. He said he didn't deserve such a good woman."

Cora's expression softened with the hint of a smile. "He doesn't," she murmured.

Dan's charm was a powerful thing, Angela noted. It was the kind of quality that used to attract her—confidence, a man who was clear on what he wanted and needed in life. Someone who enjoyed his blessings and shared them readily with others. *Focus, Angela.* She pressed the advantage. "Mrs. Guzman, has Tank told you about what is going on?"

"He's gotten into some trouble. He's going to straighten things out. It will be okay. Thanks for your concern, but we're fine."

"Did he tell you that he's afraid Harry Gruber is trying to kill him?"

Her lips thinned. "Gruber is a monster."

"How so?" Dan leaned closer. "What exactly has he done to Tank, Cora? Please tell us."

From next door, a baby wailed.

"Tank told me not to talk about it," Cora said.

"We need to know so we can help him." Dan offered another devastating smile. "All we want to do is help him and you. We're not working with Gruber. I can assure you of that. I'm a doctor and she's a chaplain, like we said. He came to Angela for help, but he ran before we got the story. Please, Cora. Tank needs us whether he knows it or not."

Cora hesitated. "Gruber knew Tank needed the money. It's wrong to take advantage of someone's desperation," she said. "That's a sin."

"Did Gruber loan Tank some money?" Angela said. "And now he wants the loan repaid?"

"He—" Cora broke off as a tan truck rumbled up the street. As the vehicle creaked toward them, Angela's chest tightened. The sign on the scratched door read "Gruber and Gruber Trucking."

It rolled closer, the silhouette familiar, the long nose, jutting chin, balding head.

The driver was Harry Gruber's brother, Peter.

Angela's palms went cold. The truck crept along until it was even with the house.

Peter did not look at them, merely inched his way along the street with excruciating slowness. The message was clear. *Watching you. Every move you make.* Cold, hard fear roiled through every muscle and nerve.

Angela heard Tank's wife suck in a breath, and then she slammed the door. The bolt grated home.

"Cora, wait," Angela called.

Silence.

They turned to watch the truck.

The unsmiling Peter gave them a grim salute as he drove away.

Dan strode to the curb, but Peter had already driven on by.

Though Angela knocked again on the door, Cora would not answer. She scrawled her cell number on the back of a business card and shoved it in the crack of the door. Dan was still staring in the direction the truck had taken.

"You know, I've always thought of Cobalt Cove as a sleepy little town, sort of a coastal Mayberry."

"And now?"

"Peter. Harry Gruber. Tank. Lila." He turned a thoughtful gaze on her. "I'm beginning to get a real bad feeling."

Though her own nerves were still hitched tight, his erect posture, the muscled shoulders and the determination on his face brought her a small measure of reassurance.

"I'm going to go back to the clinic and comb through Tank's computer records again," he said. "There wasn't much, but maybe I missed something. Lila's notes should be there, too."

She nodded, thinking that a private eye should have suggested that, but she was not a private eye. She was not even sure she was still a chaplain. The sadness of it tugged at her along with a surge of depression.

"Score one for the Grubers, but they haven't won yet." He touched her forearm in the jovial, friendly way that made her pulse kick up in spite of her good sense. "I'm starving and it's lunchtime. Want to go get a bite?"

Yes, her mind said. "No," she replied. "Um, I should go back to the hotel and wait for Marco and my sister."

"They won't be here until evening, like you said."

"I could do some computer research."

He raised a mischievous eyebrow. "You're faking, Chaplain. You don't know what to research any more than I do."

Her cheeks burned. "I…I don't like crowded places."

"Then I've got the perfect solution." He opened the passenger door with a flourish. "Onward."

She tried to find an excuse to avoid spending any more time with Dan. By the time she thought of a good reason, she was already sitting in the passenger seat, buckled in, being driven back toward the beach. The merry glint in his eyes brought back a memory, her encounter with Dan before Julio had died.

He'd been playing basketball on the makeshift court behind the hospital. She'd been on her way out after praying with a soldier who had requested her presence.

Dan had called out. "Hey, Chaplain. Need a player here. My guys are getting creamed. How about it?"

She'd laughed, declined, reconsidered and then played a vigorous game where she'd scored four baskets and earned the nickname of Swisher. He'd invited her back to play again the next day, and she'd been looking forward to it. But the next day brought bullets instead of basketball, and Julio's death.

Everything that had transpired since she had arrived in Cobalt Cove had tested the limits of her self-control. Would she have another panic attack? Run in a frenzy when the next car backfired or burst into tears at the sight of someone who looked like Julio? She imagined her humiliation at having Dan witness yet another episode. Worst of all, he knew the root of her unraveling was guilt, pure and simple. Guilt that Julio had offered up his life for hers.

She tried again to come up with an excuse, but instead she found herself relaxing in the seat as Dan turned on some music, old gospel hymns.

"Helps me think," he said. "Used to play it…" He trailed off.

In Kandahar.

Ironic, as that was when she'd stopped listening to music, the day Julio was killed. The silence grew wider and deeper until she couldn't hear from Him anymore, either.

He reached for her hand. How did he know? Why should he care?

Still, she let his warm palm remain cupping her fingers until they pulled up, once again, at the beach.

Dan purchased two Red Rocket hot dogs from Bill, the heavyset vendor with his graying hair pulled neatly back into a ponytail.

"Hey, Doc Man," Bill said as he handed over the food. He jutted a chin at Angela, who stood a few feet away, making a phone call. "That's the minister lady?"

"Chaplain," he said. "How did you know that?"

"Small town," Bill said. "News travels fast. I hear everything."

"Yeah?" Dan said. "What do you know about Harry Gruber?"

Bill's smile stayed in place, but Dan thought he detected a stiffening in the man's wide shoulders. "Runs a trucking company. They transport back and forth from Mexico and all that. Opened the clinic here a year or so ago. Brother's a dentist at the clinic."

"I already knew that part."

He shrugged. "Gruber funds the clinic. He's a good guy, right?"

"You tell me."

"Sure. Good guy."

Dan held Bill's gaze with his own. "What's the real story, Bill?"

"Real story is I'm a hot dog vendor and that's all. I got no gossip to spread, huh?" A couple of bodyboarders strode up, wetsuits unzipped and speckled with sand. Dan stepped back to allow them to order. He wasn't going to get anything further from Bill.

Angela accepted the foil-wrapped dog with a polite thank you, and they helped themselves to condiments. He was amused to see that she piled on everything from jalapeños to sauerkraut. He stuck with mustard, swathing the thing in extra napkins to avoid any mess. They scored his favorite spot on a bench overlooking the cove. The shore was still busier than usual with out of towners who had come to enjoy Beach Fest and decided to make a weekend of it, but it was quieter than a restaurant would be and that was better for her.

The wind whipped at Angela's hair, and she tried

to keep it out of her towering hot dog mess. Her laughter was warm, light and airy like the sprays of foam that danced above the waves. He handed over a napkin to catch the condiments that threatened to slide off the hot dog.

"I guess I got greedy," she said. "I'm not actually hungry enough to eat all this, but old habits die hard. My dad used to take us to watch the Padres play and he said a proper hot dog was merely a platform for all the toppings you could fit on top."

"Sounds like my kind of guy. I'd love to meet him."

A shadow darkened her green eyes to olive. "He's dead. He was murdered just before Christmas."

Dan nearly dropped his hot dog. "I didn't know. I'm sorry. Did you… Was the murderer caught?"

"Yes, and that's a blessing, but it still doesn't bring my dad back." She sighed. "That's why I'm part of this investigation thing. It was my dad's business. It just felt right to help keep it running. It means the world to my sisters."

"I get it."

After a few moments, Angela walked over to the trash and threw away her half-eaten hot dog.

He felt like kicking himself for asking to meet her father. The memory of her laugh lingered. *You will find joy again, Angela*, he wanted to tell her. *Someday.*

She stood with her face to the wind, looking out

onto the water. For a moment, he imagined himself putting his arms around her, sheltering her body with his. What would her hair feel like, whisking against his face? The soft curve of her shoulders tucked in his embrace? Then he blinked back to reality.

"Ready to go to the clinic?"

She nodded, and they retraced their steps back to the parking lot.

They passed Bill, wreathed in steam from his hot dogs. As they went by, Bill ducked his head and began wiping down his cart with vigor. No smile. No eye contact.

Gruber was a good guy?

Instinctively Dan moved closer to Angela.

Yeah. Right.

Dan let them into the darkened clinic with his key. "Closed on Sundays," he said. "The building used to be the old Cobalt Cove library, and the hospital in town was a college. Eventually they built a nice library there, too." The clinic was a three-story structure with ornate molding along the roofline and a redbrick front. The first floor had been turned into a reception room, lined with filing cabinets.

"Second floor is the clinic where we see patients for minor injuries and basic health care. Third floor is divided between dental and eye care. Three doctors total, two opticians and one dentist—that's Peter Gruber."

"So Peter and the other doctors on the third floor are private practice?"

"Yes, but they all do pro bono work on Saturdays for the clinic. Lila donates her time during the clinic days. Peter pays her for the rest."

"That's kind."

"Yeah. The clinic was started up about ten years ago by a church group, and Harry took over the funding of it last year when they couldn't continue. After his wife died, he bought the building, set his brother up on the third floor, along with the eye doctors, and he lets the clinic operate rent-free on the second floor."

"Why?"

Dan frowned. "Up until now, I'd say it was a philanthropic gesture, but I'm not sure anymore."

"Harry has no love of doctors," she mused. "You sure he doesn't make money off it somehow?"

"Not off the clinic. The private practice guys pay rent, but Harry funds the clinic."

He led her to the stairs. "I've got a cubicle office upstairs where I keep my own files." He flicked the light switch. Nothing happened. "That bulb goes out all the time. I think it's wiring in this old building. I keep meaning to fix it myself."

He heard the smile in her voice in spite of the darkness. "Are you any good at electrical stuff?"

"I can restart a heart," he said, a touch indignantly. "How hard can it be to rewire a lightbulb?"

Her soft laugh told him that it had been an arrogant statement, and he shot her a rueful smile. He heard AnnaLisa's voice in his memory.

"You're a surgeon, not a superhero."

Deep down, he didn't believe it. When he held a scalpel in his hands, he felt the power, given straight from God. The power to heal if he was only clever enough, to save lives if his fingers were agile enough. His gut throbbed.

And the ability to let a life slip away, in spite of his extreme effort.

You're only as good as God allows you to be, hotshot.

And sometimes, he was not good enough. Not a superhero. Not even a good enough surgeon to save a life. Not good enough to save Julio's.

Angela clasped his arm. He realized he must have been lost in thought. "Sorry."

She gave him a squeeze. "Glad I'm not the only one who wanders away sometimes."

He straightened. "Let's go."

They passed a paneled opening, boarded up.

"Basement. Floods when it rains."

They headed up the darkened stairs, holding on to the old wood railing to feel their way up. Emerging onto the second floor, he was about to turn on the lights when he froze.

A whirring sound echoed through the still space.

"What is that?" Angela whispered.

"A shredder."

"From the third floor? Does anyone work Sundays?"

"Not to my knowledge. I'm going to go up and see," he whispered. "Stay here."

"I'm going, too."

He wanted to argue, but instead he continued on, Angela following. The old wood stairs creaked in spite of their care. He winced, hoping the sound of the shredder would cover their progress.

The grinding of the shredder grew louder. He could feel Angela tense behind him. He put out a hand. She gripped his palm, her skin icy to his touch.

He wanted to reassure her, but he didn't want to risk alerting the Sunday shredder of their presence.

They moved up another step, and the wood creaked loudly under Dan's weight. The sound of the shredder ceased abruptly.

She crept up onto the step next to him, mouth close to his ear.

Whatever she was about to say, he never heard. The door slammed open and Dan was yanked off his feet and pulled into the darkened office.

EIGHT

Angela stumbled forward, clutching for Dan. She ricocheted off the slammed door. Reeling, she fell backward, tumbling down three steps before she could regain her balance, banging her elbows and shoulder into the hard wood railing. Panting, she righted herself.

"Dan," she yelled as she charged back up the steps, slamming palms first into the stairwell door. It was locked. She pounded on it, screaming. "Answer me!"

There was no response. Pressing her ear to the cold metal she heard a muffled crash. Throwing her shoulder at the panel did nothing. Shut tight. Without stopping to think, she ran back down the stairs to the first floor on shaky legs. Tumbling out into the reception area, gasping for breath, she dialed the police.

"I need help." She gave the address.

"What is the nature of your emergency?" the dispatcher inquired.

"There's an intruder at the medical clinic and a doctor's in trouble. Please hurry." It was the best she could manage. She knew her voice was high and tight, edging into the panicked range.

"We will send someone right away. Exit the building and stay on the line, ma'am."

But Dan was locked on the third floor. Hurt? Unconscious? Was Harry Gruber up there? His brother? Was Tank? Her mind spun with so many thoughts it dizzied her. The minutes ticked by in a whirling confusion. Fighting against the paralysis that gripped her body, she forced herself into action.

She ran to the elevator, slamming a hand onto the button. The seconds ticked by as the machine creaked on its way to meet her.

Her mind shrieked at her to run, to flee. She was walking helpless into a trap, to certain capture. A gleam of brass from the receptionist's desk caught her eye, the blade of a letter opener.

Not helpless. Not that. Hardly daring to let herself think it through, she snatched up the blade. Would she be able to use it? To stab someone? Her skin was prickled in goose bumps. When the elevator door opened, she leaped through, punching the third-floor button.

As she clutched the makeshift knife tightly, her heart hammered a violent rhythm against her chest. What was she thinking? What did she plan on doing when the elevator reached its destination? How could she protect herself and Dan with a letter opener?

Terror circled high and tight in her chest. She heard roaring, but she could not tell if it was the memories of the past or the slamming of her own pulse through her veins.

The elevator reached the second floor. Waves of sensation rippled through her, leaving her nauseous and shaking. It was dark save for the weak lighting and the gleam of the buttons marking her ascent. Shadows crowded her vision, and she thought she might pass out. Then the elevator would deliver her unconscious into the hands of her enemy. *Breathe, Angela. Keep breathing.*

What had she done? Whoever was on the top floor would be waiting for her inevitable arrival. Waiting and ready.

She reached for the buttons to hit the emergency stop, to reconsider, but the machine was already making its way to the third floor.

What if Dan was...?

She swallowed hard. God help me, she tried to say, but the words stayed stuck in the mire of her fear. There was only terror, which had begun to override her senses.

The letter opener trembled in her hand, and the metal walls seemed to close in on her. She realized she was pressed against the back elevator wall, breath shallow and rapid, palms ice-cold.

Ding.

The elevator doors slid open. She did not move. Through the gap she could see nothing but a darkened office, empty and quiet. Her hand jerked toward the close-door button. *Run, get away, live*, her body screamed.

But Dan?

Where was he? Could she flee and leave him there? Would he die like Julio for getting involved with her?

In a rush, on trembling legs, she stepped out into the office.

She listened over the roaring of the blood through her veins. The elevator doors slid closed behind her. Cut off now. No escape the way she had come.

It was silent at first.

Then the squeak of metal. She edged forward past a cubicle where there stood an empty exam chair. Trays of dental tools, wrapped and sterile sat waiting for the next patient. She passed a second cubicle, also empty. The squeak sounded again, louder.

In the far corner of the office was a final cubicle. It was dark and quiet, save for a soft scuffling coming from that space. In vain she listened for the sound of approaching sirens. Forcing in a breath, she willed her feet to move closer. Each step drove the fear to new heights.

Help him, Angela. Help Dan.

One more step and she peeked in the cubicle.

Dan was slumped in a chair, someone bending

over him. He was unresponsive, injured in some way, perhaps bound?

"Don't touch him," she ordered.

The bending figure straightened. It was Peter Gruber.

"The police are almost here," she said. "Get away from him."

Peter's face remained expressionless, but he held up his hands, palms toward her, and did as she asked. Keeping a close watch on Peter, she edged closer to Dan and grabbed his shoulder.

"Dan?"

He groaned and stirred. She could see a developing bruise on his cheekbone. Hurt but alive. The relief almost choked her.

Peter leaned on the edge of his desk, watching her. He was taller than his brother; his thinning hair was on its way to matching Harry's bald dome. Everything from the shape of the nose to the cock of the head marked them as siblings.

She wished her hands were not shaking so badly. "What did you do to him?"

"I pulled him into the office, and he smacked his head on the desk. I was about to check his pupils when you arrived."

"Why are you here?"

"I work here. Why are you here?" A hint of anger threaded through. "I thought you were some derelict trying to break into the office. That's why

I yanked open the door and grabbed Dan. You shouldn't be here."

Dan groaned again and opened one eye. Blinking, he shook his head. "Angela?"

She squeezed his shoulder. "You okay?"

"Yeah." He touched his cheekbone gingerly, eyeing Peter. "You could have just opened the door and asked what we were doing."

"And you could have called on the phone and arranged to speak to me like a normal person."

"We've got reasons not to trust you," Dan said. "You were driving past Cora's house earlier, scaring her."

"I was being cautious. Lots of kids in the streets. You've got to be careful with kids."

"What were you doing in Harry's truck?" she said.

"I help my brother out doing deliveries when I can. Clean his teeth, too." A hint of a smile. "I'm a dentist, you know." He said to her, waving a hand around. "Hence the dental office."

She still clung to the letter opener. There was no way she was going to trust Peter Gruber any more than she trusted Harry.

Torrey and another officer pounded up the stairs, hands on their guns. Breathing hard, Torrey crossed the floor. "What's going on?"

"I came to check on something. Heard what I thought was an intruder," Dan said.

"They sneaked up the stairwell and I figured it

was a burglar." Peter shrugged. "I knocked him off his feet and dragged him into the office and slammed the door." He smirked. "I think I defended myself pretty handily against two people breaking and entering."

"It wasn't breaking and entering. I have a key," Dan said.

Torrey lowered his gun. "Working on a Sunday, Dr. Gruber?"

Peter shrugged.

"And you, Dr. Blackwater? Decided to put in a few hours tidying up some paperwork?"

Dan stared at Peter. "I guess we're both hard workers."

"I guess so," Peter said.

Gruber did not look in the least nonplussed. "About time you got here, Torrey," he said.

"Came as soon as we got the call."

Angela glanced at the paper shredder and the file next to it with the neat label *Guzman*. "Why were you shredding this file?"

She heard a soft sound behind her, the turning of a knob as the door to a small storage room opened.

She gasped in shock when Lila Brown stepped out.

"He wasn't," she said. "I was."

Dan tried hard to focus in spite of the pain throbbing in his face. Lila was dressed in baggy clothes a couple sizes too big for her. She was pale, lips chapped.

"Why did you run from the hospital?"

"I got tired of being there. Checked myself out," she said.

"That's not true." Angela put down the letter opener she was holding. "Someone sent you flowers and a lock of hair in an envelope."

"Are we back to that again?" Torrey said.

Lila stood stiffly. "I don't know what you're talking about."

"It was the Grubers, wasn't it?" Angela said. "They're trying to scare you. Are they threatening to hurt your son?"

"My son is nobody's business but mine." Lila snatched the file from Angela's hand. "I checked myself out. I resigned my job here, so I came to tidy up. Dr. Gruber was here working, too. He... persuaded me not to quit."

"How did he do that?" Angela said. "By scaring you?"

Peter's face remained expressionless, but his eyes hardened like two flints. "By offering her a raise. She's a good employee. I don't want to lose her."

Angela picked up the folder. "And this file? You just happen to be shredding Tank's information? The day after you were begging him not to meet with me? I heard you on the phone—remember?"

"You misunderstood."

"No, I didn't."

"Someone tried to blow you up," Dan said. "Lila, if you're scared, let us help you."

"Or the cops," Torrey said. "That's what we're paid to do."

"I'm fine," she said. "I just want to be left alone."

"No you're not fine. You're being threatened. Blackmailed."

Peter cleared his throat. "She said she's not. What evidence do you have to the contrary?"

Dan got to his feet, pain throbbing. "You and your brother scared her in the hospital. You know it and we know it."

"You're looking at the wrong people here. Tank is the bad guy." Peter folded his arms.

"Peter," Lila started.

"No. I'm not going to protect him." Peter's eyes narrowed into angry slits. "Tank's a drug user and a thief. He's infatuated with Lila and he won't leave her alone. If there are any threats being leveled at her, it's from Tank, not me or my brother."

"Is that true, Lila?" Torrey said. "What about the stairwell? Did Peter or his brother, Harry, detain you in the stairwell? Or threaten you in any way?"

"No," she said.

"But—" Angela started.

"I called Peter, and he and Harry came to get me from the hospital. I asked them not to tell anyone, so they were lying to protect me. I'm sorry if it caused problems."

"It didn't," Peter said. "You were right to be

scared of Tank, and Harry and I would do anything to protect you. Did he send you the flowers and card?"

Her mouth tightened, and she stared at him for a moment. "I don't know who sent the flowers, and I never saw any card."

"You don't need to protect Tank or be scared of him," Peter said, covering her hand with his. "We're going to keep you safe."

She offered a tremulous smile before she pulled away.

"Is it true that Tank is infatuated with you?" Torrey said.

"We're just friends. That's all."

Peter moved closer. "She's a loyal person and she doesn't want to get him in trouble."

Lila nodded. "Yes," she whispered. "I don't want any trouble with anyone."

Torrey radioed dispatch and filled them in. "Still, Miss Brown, I'd like to talk to you if you don't mind. Just a few questions."

She nodded, her gaze avoiding Peter Gruber.

When Torrey led Lila away to an empty cubicle, Peter fixed a final look on Angela and Dan. "My brother is a good man. He puts a big chunk of his profits into this clinic because he believes that everyone should have the same access to health care. He's a hero, not a monster."

"What about you?" Dan said. "Just a nice guy

who happens to be driving along in front of Cora Guzman's house?"

Peter's expression hardened. "Look. All I want is to keep Lila safe from Tank Guzman. He's been terrorizing Lila, stalking her. I wanted to show him what it feels like when the woman he loves feels uncomfortable."

The woman he loves?

Angela cocked her head. "Peter, are you in love with Lila Brown?"

Peter jerked and raised his hand, cheeks flushing. "Me? Of course not. I'm her boss. She's a good worker and she's my friend. I care about her—that's all. I've got to go call my brother now and tell him what's just gone on at his clinic." He turned on his heel and stalked away.

Angela watched him go. "Who is telling the truth?"

Dan couldn't answer. Gingerly, he followed Angela back down the stairs, and they stood for a moment in the sunlit parking lot.

"This is spinning out of control," Angela said. "Everyone's got a different story."

"One thing's for sure—Lila's still scared."

"But is she scared of Harry or Tank? Or Peter?"

"That's too many questions for me right now. My head is throbbing."

"You should go to a doctor."

"And have my head examined?" He laughed.

"It's like a big block of cement. Perfectly fine." On impulse, he caught up Angela's hand and kissed it.

"What's that for?"

"You came back for me after I conked my head."

She shook her head mournfully. "If Peter's telling the truth, he wasn't intending to hurt you. There never was any danger, except in my mind."

"You didn't know that. You grabbed a letter opener and came after me, all by yourself."

"Some rescue," she said, rubbing her free palm on the leg of her jeans as if to rub away the feel of the letter opener.

"Some courage," he echoed. "You were brave."

For a moment, her eyes glimmered, then she looked away, detaching herself. "I'm not brave, Dan."

"I beg to differ."

The sun drifted behind a cloud, and her eyes went from emerald to sage. "I'm so scared I can't do my job. I can't even pray."

"God's patient. He'll wait until you're ready."

"I don't think I will be. I'm…" She gulped. "I'm going to ask to be discharged." She breathed hard. "I can't serve. I can't help people."

"You helped me just now."

She blinked hard again. "My last assignment, before I was put on leave…I was supposed to escort a family to view their son who'd been killed by an IED and flown home." She stopped.

"You couldn't do it?" he said softly.

"I couldn't even get out of the car," she spat, hitting every word hard. "I stayed there, clutching the steering wheel, crying like a kid. I was supposed to be there comforting, helping that family hold on to their faith and I couldn't even get the seat belt off." Her laugh was bitter. "How's that for a chaplain? Crying in the front seat while a family waited to say good-bye to their son. That's not serving."

He tried to take her hand, but she pulled away.

"Don't call me brave, Dan. Please. It's an insult to all the men and women we served with."

The silence built between them for a few moments. "If you were counseling someone who felt the way you do, would you tell them they were a coward?" He kept his voice low and soft. "Or would you tell them they'd been injured and they needed help?"

"Don't you see? I wouldn't tell them anything," she said, voice breaking, one tear edging down her face. "I can't hear God anymore, Dan, so what right have I to counsel anyone else?"

"Angela—" he started.

The words came out in a halting whisper. "I can't hear God anymore," she breathed, trembling.

"With time and help, you will. He hasn't left you."

She sucked in a deep breath. "I'm going to walk back to my hotel."

"I'll drive you."

She shook her head, bangs trailing in front of those haunted green eyes. "I need to walk."

He watched her leave, head down, hands jammed into her pockets as she shuffled along. Sorrow for her made him ache inside. He looked up at the sky, to the puff of clouds against a brilliant blue.

"Help her, Lord. Find Your way through that silence and restore her connection with You."

Another cloud darkened the sun. Dan watched its progress, his gaze going to the third-floor window. Peter Gruber looked down, following Angela's progress like a cat tracking a wounded bird.

Something went cold and hard inside Dan, a surge of protectiveness rippling through his gut. Angela had been hurt enough. He turned and stepped away from the building, staring right back up at Peter, sending the message loud and clear.

If you think you're going to intimidate her, you've got another think coming.

NINE

Angela locked herself in her hotel room and closed the curtains. She wanted nothing more than to hide from the world, from feelings that she could not control, pulsing unexpectedly like the flames of a wind-whipped fire.

At the core of it, she was afraid. Of losing control, of the threats she saw building all around her from the Grubers and Tank. But most of all, she feared that her soul would be trapped in this dark place forever.

Dan was right. If she was ministering to a soldier in the same situation, she would tell him that he'd been injured and he needed help for his PTSD. And she'd tried to get it for herself, but the shame and despair had made her discontinue seeing the doctor after only two visits. The final humiliation had been encountering a soldier she'd supported waiting to see the same doctor that she was. How could she counsel when she couldn't find comfort herself? And how could she talk to others about God when He was silent in her life?

She closed her eyes, drifting off into a troubled sleep until a knock on the door made her leap to her feet, pillow clutched to her chest. A quick glance at the clock told her it was late afternoon, almost four.

"Angela?" Marco's deep voice called. "Are you in there?"

She unlocked the door. Marco and Donna stood there, bags in hand.

Donna threw her arms around Angela and she endured the hug, disentangling herself as quickly as she could.

"I was getting worried when you didn't answer," Donna said. She was tanned and trim, long mane of hair highlighted from her time honeymooning in the sun.

"Why aren't you with Brent?" Angela said.

She laughed. "Disasters don't take vacations, so neither does the coast guard. He's deployed to help with the evacuations on a distressed oil tanker, so I've got a week apart from my new hubby and the veterinary office."

Angela was happy to see the smile on her sister's face when she spoke of her husband. Brent was a fine man, and Donna deserved nothing less.

Marco bent to kiss Angela on the cheek. His dark eyes took in every detail of her face. "Your mother said I was to ask you if you've been getting enough to eat."

Angela quirked a smile. "And what are you supposed to do about it if the answer is no?"

Marco shifted. "I figured Donna could handle that part." He sat in a chair, Donna on the small sofa while Angela filled them in on the events since she'd arrived. She did not add anything about her emotional mess. That wasn't something they needed to know.

Marco sat and listened, forearms leaning on his knees as he absorbed every detail without interrupting. Donna showed no such restraint, peppering Angela with questions until she reached the end with Peter at the clinic office.

"So who's the bad guy here?" Donna said. "Tank? Peter? Harry? The cop?"

"That's why I called you." Angela sighed. "I don't know."

Marco raised a thick eyebrow. "What's the doc think?"

She looked at her hands, but she knew Marco was watching for her reaction, gauging how deeply Dan was involved.

"He's unsure."

Marco waited a beat. "Is he going to be a part of this?"

Was he? Angela could not bear the calculating gleam in her sister's eye. If only they knew how completely unable she was to be involved in a relationship of any kind. But then, she'd kept them as far away from her problems as she could. "It's possible. He considers Lila Brown a friend, and she's definitely scared of someone."

Donna twisted a strand of her long hair. "Dan served with you, Candace said. Do we count him as a friend?"

"When he proves himself to be," Marco said.

Always the gruff exterior, Marco was also a man who loved deeply and cared about the Gallagher family since he had none of his own anymore.

"First step is background checks on the players," Marco said. "Grubers, Lila Brown, Tank Guzman."

"I don't think Tank is the guilty party here."

"Is that because you don't want him to be?" Donna asked with typical Gallagher bluntness.

Angela bit back an angry remark. "No. He brought me into this mess because he thinks we can prove Harry Gruber is trying to kill him."

"Why?" Donna's eyes rolled in thought. "How would a down-on-his-luck, unemployed guy be a threat to Harry Gruber? Gruber's a successful business man, a philanthropist. Guzman's a nobody."

"He's not a nobody," Angela snapped. Marco and Donna stared. She took a breath. "I'm sorry. I know you didn't mean it that way. I want to help him. I think he's telling the truth."

Donna's face was still troubled. "Okay. You know him better than we do. Still, we'll see what we can turn up on all three of them, okay?"

Angela nodded.

"Mind if I bunk here with you?" Donna said. "Marco's got a room across the hall."

As much as she loved her sister, Angela did not want to have anyone around. But there seemed no way out of it that would not hurt Donna's feelings and incur unnecessary expense.

"Sure."

Marco and Donna decided to get some dinner at the Beachbum, but Angela declined. When she was finally alone, she sat on the edge of the bed, trying to put her spiraling thoughts in order. It was a huge comfort to have Marco and Donna in Cobalt Cove. Then why was her stomach still doing backflips?

Of all the details whirling in her mind, the one she could not forget was the lock of downy hair. Both Lila and Peter denied it had ever been there. So did the orderly. But she had seen it and so had Lila, and whoever sent it knew it would terrorize Lila into doing whatever they wanted of her.

Peter said Tank was infatuated with Lila. And her child, too?

What was Tank's connection to Lila, anyway?

She suddenly realized how very little she knew about either one of them, how very little she knew about any of it.

The following morning Dan watched the sun rise in its glorious splendor over the still waters of Cobalt Cove as he munched his way through a bowl of granola and poured some cat food in a bowl for

Babs. The air was crisp, the sky thick with wispy fog that might or might not burn off later in the day. A ping from his phone reminded him he had a noon appointment with Jeb for physical therapy. He would go for sure. Get the hand back into action and resume his role as a private-practice surgeon at the hospital.

His fingers curved as if they, even now, held the delicate instruments, the incredible telescopic cameras, the console controls that directed the robotic surgeries. The procedures were methodical, meticulously planned.

His heart traveled back to Kandahar, where no appointments were made, any plans tossed out the window at the beep of a pager that announced the arrival of the wounded. As a Role 3 hospital, they got the most critical cases and they'd saved countless lives. A navy reservist, Dan had volunteered, and all his research and preparation for what might occur was not even close to reality.

He recalled one nineteen-year-old soldier who had sustained grievous injuries to both legs, a big capital *T* written in marker on his forehead indicating he'd been brought in wearing a tourniquet. Under his uniform, he wore a ragged T-shirt with his son's handprints on either side of a pink painted heart. *I love you, Daddy.*

Dan took the tiny notebook from his pocket and trailed his finger over the neatly written names until he found the one he sought, the daddy who'd lain on Dan's table that day while a team of doctors worked feverishly to save him. A. Manning.

The *A* was for Anton, he'd learned later.

"We're going to take care of you, son," Dan had said that day in the operating theater, tainted with the smell of sweat and antiseptic.

Anton had smiled exactly one time and put his hand on Dan's sleeve. Dan had not saved Anton Manning, in spite of his own efforts and those of the crack surgical team. They had not been enough. He'd mumbled his own prayer hours later as he sat with Manning's flag-draped body, making sure he was not alone while they waited for mortuary affairs to arrive. They must never be alone, the ones that had not made it. Never. Then the solemn lines of personnel formed to deliver A. Manning on his way. The final salute.

I love you, Daddy. Words Anton never heard again this side of heaven.

Dan realized he'd been staring out the window so long, his coffee was cold. He dumped it in the sink. The ache still remained, a clear sign that he had to put away the notebook and bring himself back to the present. He did so.

The task at hand: How could he help Angela and Lila?

"Bull by the horns, Blackwater," he told himself as he grabbed a jacket and headed to his truck. His plan was simple and straightforward. He'd known Lila for six months, and he figured that entitled him to a certain level of pushiness. If she was being harassed by the Grubers or Tank, maybe she'd open up to him about it. He thought about Peter staring at Angela from his office window. The only way to help her was to get to the bottom of the mystery.

He knew where Lila's home was, a small rented in-law unit out back of a residence in the next town over, Seacliff. The name of the town was more scenic than it deserved, at least the neighborhood Lila lived in, which was a good five blocks from the beach. Her unit was attached to a two-story house with a fenced-off front yard and a half-dozen small children playing there. The home owner, Mrs. Grayson, ran a day care out of her house and provided supervision for Lila's son, Quinn. All this, he'd learned in the coffee break room at the clinic.

A blue SUV was parked at the curb near the house with three people inside.

Dan parked and approached the vehicle. Marco saw him coming and rolled down the window.

"You're the doc?"

"Call me Dan. Good to meet in person."

"Likewise."

Angela sat in the backseat, looking very surprised to see him. A woman with long blond hair and the same full-lipped smile as Angela's got out of the car along with Marco.

"I'm Donna Mitchell, Angela's sister."

Dan greeted her and Marco with a warm handshake. "I don't suppose it's coincidence that we all wound up here this morning?"

Marco leaned against the car. He was a solid six feet of muscle, four inches shorter than Dan but broader around the chest. Tough guy. Dan found himself straightening as they took each other's measure.

"Wanted to talk to Lila Brown away from the clinic," Marco said.

"Good idea, but this isn't the way to do it."

Marco raised an eyebrow. "Yeah?"

"Yeah. She's scared. A bunch of strangers trooping into her home isn't going to make her want to talk."

Donna grinned. "We're very persuasive."

"That's what I'm afraid of. I'll talk to her alone."

Marco's gaze drifted to the children. "No offense, but you might not ask the right questions."

"Because I'm not a private investigator?" Dan felt a flash of irritation. "Doctors are pretty good detectives, too, for your information."

Marco shrugged.

"He didn't mean you're not qualified," Donna said.

"Yes, he did," Dan said. "But I get the point. I'm going to talk to her, but Angela should come with me. Lila's seen her face before. She can ask whatever you want her to."

Angela's eyes widened. "Lila doesn't trust me. She was trying to keep Tank away from me."

"Possibly."

Mrs. Grayson emerged in the yard, sipping a cup of coffee and staring at them.

"We're attracting attention. Come on, Angela." Dan took her by the hand before she could object and walked toward the yard. He figured if Marco and Donna were going to follow, at least he'd get a head start. They didn't.

"Marco always so direct?"

Angela sighed. "Pretty much. He's the kind of guy people love or can't stand."

It was clear that Angela and Donna adored Marco. He felt an unexpected twinge of jealousy.

Dan greeted Mrs. Grayson with a smile. "Hello, ma'am. I'm Dr. Blackwater. I'm a friend of Lila's. May I speak with her a moment?"

Mrs. Grayson looked him over. "Why?"

"Just some clinic business. It will only take a minute."

"Lila's pretty shy. She keeps to herself."

Dan applied some more genial conversation until Mrs. Grayson waved a hand. "She's out back. Go ahead."

Dan and Angela picked their way across the crooked stepping-stones and out to the tiny unit. They heard a child cry and a woman's voice singing a song about monkeys in trees. He knocked.

The singing stopped.

"Who is it?"

Dan explained.

"I'm…not feeling well," Lila said. "I can't talk to you now."

Dan exchanged a look with Angela. "We know that you're scared, Lila. Whoever put that bomb in your car meant business. We need to figure it out before you…or your baby gets hurt."

A long silence. He thought they were going to have to go back to the car and report their failure, when slowly the door creaked open. He got a glimpse of a small room, baby toys scattered on the carpet. Behind Lila was a little boy, holding himself up by gripping her pant leg, two fingers stuck in his mouth.

"Hey there," Dan said, bending down. "You must be Quinn."

Lila's face softened, but she did not open the door any farther. "Yes. He's ten months old today."

"Handsome," Angela said. "What a cutie."

Quinn had his mother's dark hair and winning smile.

"May we come in and talk?" Dan said. "Just for a minute."

Lila flinched. "Um, I don't think that's a good idea."

"Lila if you're scared of the Grubers—" Dan said.

"I'm not," she snapped. "The Grubers have been good to me. Everything is fine. Really. I don't need any help."

"You were almost blown up," Angela said. "What if your baby had been in the car?"

"He wasn't," she hissed. Then she took a calming breath. "I'm not in danger anymore. Thank you for your concern, but I want you to leave now."

"I think you are in trouble still," Dan said. "You've got to talk to someone, for your son's sake."

Eyes flashing, she swept Quinn up in her arms. "Don't tell me how to mother my son, Dr. Blackwater. You don't know anything about me or my boy. If you want to help, keep Tank away from me. As long as he's nowhere near me, we'll be fine."

"Why?" Dan pressed. "Is Tank the one who blew up your car and sent the flowers in the hospital?"

"I said I don't want to talk about it."

"I know you ran into the Grubers when you fled the hospital," Angela said. "What did they say to you?"

"Like I said, the Grubers are helping me. That's all." She started to close the door. "I'm not talking anymore. Just keep Tank away from me."

The door slammed, and they heard the lock slide home.

Dan was about to knock on the door again when he heard a shout from the street. They jogged back to the car, past a curious Mrs. Grayson.

Donna was emerging up the slope near the road. She ran for the car. Marco was nowhere in sight.

"What happened?" Angela demanded as they hurried after her sister.

"Tank showed up, at least we think it was Tank based on your description, hair long in the back, baseball cap, jacket. He was headed for Lila's house when he saw us. Marco tried to talk to him, but he took off, and Marco chased him that way. "Get in. He's headed toward the beach."

"I'll go on foot," Dan said, sprinting away from the road and down toward the weed-filled ravine where Marco had gone. He pushed through the knee-high grass, burrs clinging to his socks and jeans. The ravine abruptly ended, dumping out onto an empty parking lot that he crossed in a matter of moments. On the far side, a swirling trail of dust indicated Marco had taken a dirt path. Dan hurried after, catching sight of Marco some fifty feet ahead of him, legs churning, running hard.

Dan put on the speed and closed the gap, plenty of IRONMAN-training runs making the effort easy for him. The road climbed up to a bluff that overlooked a wide grassy lot, strewn with rusted cars and blocks of broken cement. It was some sort of dumping ground by the looks of it, with the remnants of a burned-out warehouse overlooking the mess. Birds picked around in the weeds. A rat crouched in the sun on a rusting fender.

Marco was standing near an ancient overturned truck, doing a slow circle, grumbling softly to himself.

"Lost him?" Dan said.

"He's here," Marco murmured. "I'll find him."

Donna appeared, panting. Her eyes were wild as she looked behind her. "Where is Angela?"

Dan's gut tightened down into a fist.

Marco tensed. "Thought she was with you."

"She was. We got out together, but Angela went back to the car to get her phone. I just noticed she wasn't behind me, so I ran back and checked. She's not there."

Dan scanned the machine cemetery for any sign of Angela. Nothing. Had she caught sight of Tank and taken off on her own? No, he reassured himself. Donna had just missed her somehow.

And then he heard the scream.

TEN

Angela's scream was cut off abruptly as the trail gave out underneath her and she tumbled down the slope, her phone flying out of her hand. After some dizzying rolls, she ended up lying behind a hulking camper shell scabbed over with rust, at the bottom of the hill from where she'd returned to the car to retrieve her phone. *Would it hurt you to watch your step, Angela?*

Sucking in a breath, she lay there a moment to assess. As the dizziness subsided, she chided herself. It seemed as though she'd sustained nothing worse than a scraped elbow and having the wind driven out of her.

Sitting up, she hauled herself to her feet and began searching for her phone. Thick grass and clumps of dead leaves made the search more difficult. Something flickered in the trees to her left. She froze. *Tank?* Her breathing seemed loud in her own ears. Another crack of branches.

A deer and her baby meandered out, chomping

up mouthfuls of grass. Letting out a relieved sigh that startled the deer into retreating, she bent over, trying to figure out which direction her phone had taken as it sailed through the air.

Scooting nearer to the pile of worn wood pallets stacked some sixteen high, she continued to hunt, still on the lookout for Tank. This time it was a sound from the trees on her right. She froze, peering around the pallets until her eyes finally made him out. A man, cap covering his head, crouched behind a screen of bushes. He appeared for a moment and then shrank back into the foliage, too far away for her to see his face. Was it Tank Guzman?

She wanted to call out to him; deep down in her gut, she knew he was not a threat. Julio's brother could not have attempted murder or be guilty of stalking Lila. Firm as her convictions felt, her feelings had proven unreliable recently, and she did not want to be stupid, either. She was not about to make contact with him alone. Finally spying her phone half-hidden under a clump of grass, she bent to retrieve it. Quickly she typed in a text to Marco.

Someone in the bushes near the car. I—

A shadow fell across her face. She turned. It was too late to move as a heavy body crushed hers to the ground from behind. The air rushed from her lungs as a hand pressed the back of her head into the grass and dead leaves, fingernails digging into her scalp. Debris filled her mouth as she tried to scream. Grit peppered her eyes.

Was it Tank? Had he circled around while she summoned help?

"Stop," she tried to say, but her voice was silenced by the press of earth. The soil caked her lips.

She felt a knee poke hard into her back, and her attacker pulled her jacket up and over her head. Cool air bathed her skin where her shirt rode up, arms trapped. Fear cut at her like a razor. His weight pressed the oxygen from her lungs, and her body was frozen in horror.

Help me, she tried to yell, but nothing would pass her lips. She heard the snick of a knife being removed from its sheath; out of the corner of her eye she got a glimpse of a watch on the man's tensed wrist.

A knife. He was going to kill her.

The knowledge kick-started something inside. The urge to fight for her life nearly choked her. *No, no, no.* She shot out an elbow behind her, but the man slammed it away, sending sparks of pain through her arm.

Then she felt the point of a blade between her shoulders. He leaned close and put his mouth next to her head. She could see nothing but smothering blackness, but she felt the warmth of his breath through the denim of her jacket.

"Now you're going to die," the voice said.

She felt the knife slice into her skin, the sting of the cut, the warmth of blood welling up.

I'm going to be killed, here in this field. I'll never see my sisters again. Or Marco. Or Dan.

Terror ballooned inside and let loose a wave of strength she did not know she possessed. Jerking back, she slammed her head into the man, and she felt him reel back as her skull connected with bone. Then she was running, sprinting, fleeing without a backward glance over the grassy field, back up toward the road where she would find the others.

In the distance, she heard a voice shouting. "Angela. Where are you?"

Dan. If only she could get to him. Behind her she heard feet pounding over the uneven ground. She slipped, tripped over a hidden length of pipe, went down as hands grabbed her again.

Too winded to scream, she wriggled and struck out wildly with her feet, but now he had her by the hair. Again he reached for her jacket, fingers clawing at her back, to cover her head so he could finish the job.

She bucked and jerked, desperate to preserve her life, but it was too much, he was too strong and her adrenaline was giving way to paralyzing fear that deadened her every limb.

Oh, God, she thought, *don't let him take my life.*

He'd succeeded in covering her head again and she heard the knife being pulled free from the sheath. Then there was a brief moment when the point began to sink into her flesh.

She closed her eyes, tears springing loose from under the lids. She tried to kick out one more time, but her strength was no match for his.

"Angela," she heard Dan shout, nearer now.

And then the weight was lifted from her back as the guy took off. She wanted to raise her head, identify her attacker, but she found she did not have the strength. An odd whimpering sob was all she could manage. The ground vibrated as Dan made it to her side, Marco and Donna right behind him.

"Angie," Donna said. "Oh, Angie."

She felt gentle hands on her, helping her sit up. Dan was on his knees, peering into her eyes, his hands running over her arms.

"What did he do to you?" he croaked.

She could only stare in horror.

"Ambulance and police on their way," Marco said. "Tell us what happened, Angela."

She found she could not speak over the chattering of her teeth. Dan crawled around behind her. "Small knife wound on her back, shallow. No… signs of further injury."

Donna clutched her hand. "You're all right now, sis. You're safe."

She did not feel safe. Except for the fingers clutching hers and Dan's big hand on her shoulder she could not feel anything at all.

"When I get hold of Tank," Marco said slowly. "He's going to pay for what he did to you."

"I'm…I'm not sure it was him," she finally managed. "I never saw his face."

"We were chasing him," Marco said. "He was right ahead of us. Easy to double back. It had to be him."

"Tank has no reason to kill me. He wanted my help."

"Could be he changed his mind about talking," Donna said, wiping the dirt from Angela's face with her sleeve. "You're digging around too much, unearthing things that might incriminate him."

"I don't think it was him."

She saw the look Dan and Marco exchanged. And in a moment all her fear turned to anger. She shook off Dan's hand and got to her feet, wobbling, rubbing her jacket sleeve across her face. "It wasn't him. I don't care if you believe me or not. Tank didn't do this to me."

"Angela—" Marco started.

Dan held up a palm. "Okay. Let's say that's true. Who else could it have been?"

"Harry Gruber." The name came instinctively to her lips. "It could have been him."

Thinking about Harry with his bloodstained shirt caused her knees to tremble even more violently, and Dan and Angela insisted she sit and wait for the ambulance.

"I'm going to look around again," Marco said.

"See if I can find anything the guy dropped or left behind."

"I'll go, too, in case you need backup," Donna said. "Angie, are you going to be okay?"

She managed a nod. "Yes, go."

Dan did not try to make conversation. He sat next to her, with his arm around her shoulders. Her mind tried to make her body believe what had just happened. She'd been attacked. Someone had tried to kill her. Had it really occured? Was she in the grip of a nightmare?

But there was Dan, his warmth anchoring her to the real world, assuring her that the experience was real…and over. Before long, she found her head sagging onto his shoulder as she cried, great gulping sobs that sounded inhuman. He stood for a moment to take off his jacket and wrap it carefully around her. Then he eased down, reached for her hand and held tight until the ambulance arrived.

At the hospital, Dan made sure they cleaned and bandaged Angela's wound properly and checked for signs of shock and head injury before they ordered him into the waiting room. When they finally allowed him to see her again, he offered so many comments to the on-call doctor that the man looked at him in exasperation.

"Did you want to put on my coat and take over?"

Dan mumbled an apology. He was racked with

guilt that he had not arrived sooner to get the monster off her. As it was, if he'd been a moment later...

He swallowed and looked to greet Lieutenant Torrey. A nurse came in to clean up after the doctor. Violet, the same one who had been there when Lila ran from the hospital the day before.

"My guys are looking for physical evidence," Torrey said, "but there isn't much. Can any of you positively ID Tank Guzman as the man you were chasing?"

"Marco and Donna had never met him. The only person who saw him was Angela."

"But I couldn't see his face," she said. She'd convinced them to allow her to get dressed again, he noted. He didn't think there was any chance she was going to follow the doctor's orders and rest there for a few hours.

"And once again Guzman doesn't have the guts to show up and explain himself," Torrey said. "Just like he did after Lila Brown almost got blown to bits."

The nurse flicked a startled glance at Torrey, but he didn't notice. His cell phone buzzed, so he stepped outside to take the call.

"Violet," Dan said to the nurse. "That's your name, isn't it?"

She nodded. "Returned to work yet, Dr. Blackwater?"

He felt his cheeks warm, and suddenly he was looking out the window. He felt Angela watching him closely. "Yes, yes, I intended to start a couple of months ago, but I hurt my hand in a bicycle accident."

"Sorry to hear that," she said. Was there an echo of judgment in the tone? Or was it a product of his own discomfort at his extended leave?

He shook the thoughts away. "You've been here a long time in Cobalt Cove, Violet."

"Going on thirty-five years now. Almost ready for retirement." She grinned. "Good thing, too, my insteps aren't going to make it too much longer. Just need to add a little more to my nest egg."

"I hear you about the feet." He smiled back. "So do you know the Guzman family?"

Her look grew cautious. "My kids went to school with Julio and Tank. Good boys. Iona did her best raising them without a husband to support her."

"Do you know Lila Brown, too?"

"She didn't grow up here. Moved in as a junior, I think. Had it bad for Julio, but Iona didn't approve."

"Why?"

"Lila was a party girl. Lived with her older brother. Never did know what happened to her parents. She was into drinking and having a good time. Got kicked out of school for truancy. When Julio's grades started to suffer, Iona blamed Lila and made Julio's life miserable until he broke it off with her, or at least that's what he told his mama."

Angela looked thoughtful. "Did Lila have a relationship with Tank also?"

Violet looked away. "Gonna have to ask Iona that."

Angela's face went slack. "Iona lives nearby then?"

"Sure does. She's at a retirement home 'bout thirty miles from here. Assisted living. She had a stroke after Julio was killed."

The stress of a soldier's death rippled through so many lives, parents, siblings, spouses, friends. He shot a look at Angela, pale and staring. Navy chaplains, too. What sort of mess had Tank gotten involved in this time? He prayed it would not result in another tragedy being laid on Iona's doorstep. How much grief could one heart hold?

He looked at Angela, sitting up now, arms wrapped tightly around herself. She was only a few feet away from him, but it might as well have been a universe. How much grief could one heart hold?

Plenty, he thought.

ELEVEN

Torrey returned and gestured for Dan to join him in the hallway. "Ms. Gallagher insists it wasn't Tank who attacked her. Thinks it was Harry Gruber."

"Then I believe her."

He frowned. "I called up her CO in San Diego. She's on leave for stress."

"The CO didn't tell you that." The navy protected the privacy of its people.

"Not in so many words, but I can read between the lines."

Dan held Torrey's gaze. "If she says it was Harry Gruber that attacked her, I believe it."

"Why? Because you served with her?"

"I believe it," he repeated.

"I get it," Torrey said. "That wartime bond. My son did two tours before he got sick. Relocated here on the coast." Torrey's face grew bitter. "Guess that healing ocean air doesn't work on the kidneys."

Dan felt a surge of compassion at Torrey's bleak expression. "Bad?"

"Approaching failure. Again."

Again. There was such a heavy weight in that single world. "I'm sorry."

"Yeah. If there was a loving God up there, He would have given us a few extra kidneys." His laugh was bitter.

Realization sparked in Dan. "Did you donate a kidney to your son?"

Torrey sagged in defeat, looking at a spot somewhere over Dan's head. "No. He wouldn't take that, or anything else from me."

"He's on the transplant list?"

"Sure."

"So you've got hope then?"

Torrey shoved his hands in his jacket pocket. "Is there any other choice but to have hope for your kid?"

Dan had always dreamed of having a family. He and AnnaLisa had talked a good deal about their plans after he returned stateside, for marriage and children. She wanted to wait until she'd earned her PhD, but he'd come home impatient to marry and build a family. He'd seen so much death, witnessed how lives could be irrevocably altered in a moment, he no longer wanted to put off having kids. AnnaLisa did not feel the same urgency. He wasn't a parent, but he could still imagine there would never be a time when a father stopped holding out hope, no matter how slim, for a child's recovery. "No. I'm sure there isn't," he said.

Torrey shrugged and continued on down the hallway.

Marco and Donna were with Angela when he returned to her room.

"I'm getting out of here," Angela was saying.

"The doctors said you should stay and rest for a little while," Donna said.

"I'm leaving," Angela repeated.

Donna shot Dan a look. "Of all the sisters, she has the most common sense, but that's not playing out at the moment."

Angela grabbed her soiled jacket. "Do you know how much time I've spent in hospitals, Donna?"

Throughout her chaplaincy and her sister's injury following their father's murder, he didn't doubt she'd done a lot of time in hospitals, but at this moment, she could not do her job and it tormented her.

And him? Is that why he'd been dragging his feet about coming back? He flexed his fingers. No, it was purely a necessary delay.

"Okay. Come back to the hotel. Take a shower. Get into bed. Marco and I will keep working."

"I want to take a walk."

Donna shook her head. "Marco, you tell her."

Marco folded his arms across his muscled chest. "Sometimes it's better to be moving."

Donna shot him an aggravated look, but Dan could tell that Marco was a man who understood trauma.

Donna huffed out a breath. "All right, we'll go for a walk then."

"I've got a place on the beach," Dan said. "Great porch for sitting and a beach for walking, which I like to pretend is my own, though the town of Cobalt Cove would tend to disagree. Come over."

Angela looked as though she was going to cry. "I need to be alone."

Alone. What a dangerous place to be, both physically and spiritually, he thought.

"I'll drive you to my place and show you the beach trail," Dan said quickly. "Then I'll keep my distance."

"But—" Donna started.

Marco put a hand on her arm, eyes riveted on Dan. "We'll keep up the search for Tank. Meet up later."

Donna started to protest again, but Marco guided her to the door. He put a hand gently on the bed, not touching Angela but close.

"Right here if you need us."

She nodded but didn't look at him.

"Right here," he repeated.

Dan walked Marco and Donna out while Angela put her shoes on. Marco faced him full-on. "This beach trail?"

"I can lay eyes on it the whole time."

"I'm worried about her," Donna said. "She hasn't been the same since she came back from Afghanistan."

No one ever is, he felt like saying.

"And with my father and now this…" Donna pursed her lips in a way he'd seen Angela do. "And you're going to keep your distance?"

Dan nodded.

Marco gave him an appraising look. "Not too much distance."

He shook his head, and they reached a silent understanding right there in the bland hospital corridor.

"Going to go find out where Tank might be holing up," Marco said. They made arrangements to meet up later in the afternoon and Donna reluctantly allowed Marco to lead her away.

Not too much distance, he silently echoed. Far enough to respect Angela's wishes, but close enough that she would not be hurt again.

Angela tried to bottle up her desperate need to be outside as Dan drove her back to his house on the beach. A blanket of smothering anger enveloped her, and she was afraid it would come out via angry words that Dan did not deserve. He turned on some gospel music, and she tried to focus on the lyrics.

I stand at the door…

It took her back to that moment in church when she was fifteen years old. She remembered the pastor's voice, low and resonant, "Behold I stand at the door and knock. If any man hear My voice and open the door, I will come into him and sup with him and he with Me."

She had felt her calling so clearly from that moment forward, until that one day, that one moment when the bullets started flying. Was her faith so fragile? Had she misheard and misunderstood? Had she been an unqualified preacher, with the necessary pastoral credentials but no depth of faith when her life fell apart?

Since her time at the Navy Chaplain School at Fort Jackson some ten years prior, she'd conducted services everywhere from hospitals to the back of supply trucks to bombed-out houses. People were always surprised to know that her job involved ministering to soldiers of all faiths, helping all her charges worship. All those souls in her hands, ice-cold hands that now trembled in her lap as she got out of the car.

"Would you like to come in?" Dan asked. "Have a cup of tea or coffee?"

"No, thank you. If you'll just point me to the trail…"

"I'll walk you down. Was going to check the tarp on my kayaks, anyway. It's supposed to rain soon."

"And you want to keep an eye on me." She felt a kindling of anger, but his smile and shrug disarmed her.

"You're a good-looking gal, and I'm a red-blooded boy. Of course I'm going to want to keep my eyes on you. Who wouldn't?"

Her cheeks warmed, the only heat she could feel through her numbness. She didn't know how to respond except to follow him as he headed down the slope away from his house. The ramshackle structure surprised her. She'd pictured him in a fancy place, accomplished surgeon that he was. This was a weathered old building that would soon be in need of a new roof.

Dan walked past the house, down the slope to a dock where two kayaks were bobbing on the water. One was a double-seater. She wondered if his former fiancée had paddled the bay with him. The wind was cold, whipping her face and cheeks, and she realized her back stung where she'd been cut and her ribs ached from the pressure of the man who'd nearly killed her.

Her legs began to shake. *Don't think about it.* But her limbs started to tremble until she sank down on a bench nearest the dock. Dan did not comment but stooped over one of the kayaks. It was the double-seater.

"I think I'm going out for a paddle. Want to come?"

A paddle? Now when she'd been nearly killed? When her body felt bruised and battered? But something deep inside whispered, *Go.* And she found herself easing closer until in a few moments she was seated in the back of the kayak, a paddle in her hands. Dan tossed a waterproof blanket over her legs.

"In case you get splashed," he said.

They left the dock with a lurch. Soon he settled into a steady paddling rhythm, wide shoulders moving easily. "I can paddle for both of us," he called.

And he could; she had no doubt. Her own back stung from the attacker's wound, but the cut seemed to have etched a strong rebellion in her. As much as she wanted to run back to Coronado and hide, she would not let herself be helpless. Bad enough she could not shake the war from her mind; she would not be a victim of a homegrown thug. Where the resolve came from, she did not know. It was a new and unexpected feeling. She picked up the paddle and began to dip in the water. It took her a few moments to synchronize with Dan, but once she did the kayak moved smoothly through the water.

And what was the strange emotion she felt inside? A tiny flicker of courage. From her? A wounded woman? A useless chaplain? Inadequate to the job of investigator? To her utter astonishment, she felt an echo from long ago, a time when she had enjoyed being on the water and relished living on the exquisite California coast. It had been one of the places she'd so longed to return to during those parched days in the desert. It felt, just for a split second, as though she'd experienced a piece of home.

Cold wind buffeted her face, chilling her cheeks and making her eyes water, yet the kayak bore them on through the choppy waters of Monterey Bay and into a long narrow slough.

"If you come in the spring, you can see the snowy plovers, but there's always something amazing here no matter what the season."

She rested, taking in the rippled water, letting Dan guide the kayak near the bank where a dozen sea lions lolled, basking in the sun that poked through the clouds at irregular intervals.

Basking in the blessing. The thought startled her.

He turned. "Are—" He broke off. A look suffused his face for a moment before he hid it behind his charming smile.

"What?"

"I was going to ask if you were cold or tired."

"Did you lose your train of thought?"

"No. The sun lit up your eyes just then. I forgot how bright they were, like the color of spring."

The wonder and admiration in his expression made her blush. She pushed her hair away from her face. "I'm sure I look like a mess."

"No," he said, perfectly serious. "You are matchless."

Matchless. How could he think so? Ruined woman that she was. Failed minister. Matchless. She turned the word over and over again as she picked up her paddle and helped pilot them back to the dock, tucking away the thoughts for later. In spite of the activity, she was frozen, teeth chattering by the time they returned and tied up the boats. Dan secured the kayak under a tarp. A sprinkle of rain hit her cheek.

"Come inside and I'll make us some coffee. I'm a regular barista."

She agreed, and he led her back to the house.

The inside was sparse, tidy, with a serviceable table and chairs and a personal gym set up in the corner. There were no decorations, no extraneous frills. As Dan set about fussing with a complicated coffee machine, she wandered to the wooden shelves that housed a neat collection of comic books.

"Are you a collector?" she said in surprise.

"Yeah," he said. "Always wanted to be the hero, I guess."

"Doctors are heroes." She thought about the hundreds of lives he'd saved in Kandahar, the bodies he had snatched from the brink of death.

He sighed, pulling the levers and watching as the dark stream of coffee poured into her cup. "At the end of the day, I only get to save if that's what God wants."

"But putting yourself out there to be used," she said. "In that horrible situation," she forced the words out over a mouth suddenly gone dry. "That's not something everyone would do."

He handed her a cup, the warmth delicious on her cold fingers. "You did."

"I ran away," she blurted. *From my grief. From God.*

"We all run away sometimes, Angela," he said softly. "I think the distance reminds us that we need Him. 'If you remain in Me and I in you, you will bear much fruit; apart from Me you can do nothing.'"

Apart from Me. She turned away from his intense gaze, the rich color shimmering like the potent coffee he was brewing. He began to fiddle with some milk-steaming device. Walking to the window, she looked out on the tossing waves. "Quite a view. Is that why you bought this place?"

"Yes. I had another home in Carmel. We were building it together, AnnaLisa and I."

"Your fiancée?"

He sipped, joining her at the window. "You're wondering why we broke up, aren't you?"

"I was being polite and not asking."

He laughed. "I should try that technique. Anyway, we broke up because I came back home a different man."

"Different how?"

"After seeing what I'd seen…" His mouth tightened. "I just didn't care as much about the things I'd cared about before, my career, the fancy house, traveling. I wanted to marry and start a family, not wait anymore until our careers goals were met. It wasn't fair to change my priorities and expect that AnnaLisa would change hers. We're still friends. She's dating someone else, and I'm happy for her."

She searched his expression and found sincerity there along with a small measure of regret.

"Did you come back a better man?" she asked.

He pursed his lips, the action throwing his strong profile into shadow. She loved the way he considered the question. The answer, she knew, would be honest, even if it wasn't what she wanted to hear.

The rumble of a motorcycle startled them both.

"Uh-oh," Dan said, checking his watch. "Missed another one."

"Missed another what?"

With a resigned sigh, he walked to the door as a heavyset man, probably somewhere in his midsixties, got off his motorcycle. The ancient bike had an attached sidecar from which a black Lab hopped out, scooting to the man's side.

The man was out-and-out glowering as he stalked up the drive.

"Who is that?" she whispered.

"That's my physical therapist, Jeb Paulson."

"He makes house calls?"

"Only for his AWOL patients. I think I'm about to be court-martialed, or maybe drawn and quartered."

Jeb pounded on the door.

Angela could not hold back a smile at the doomed look on Dan's face as he went to open it.

TWELVE

Jeb did not wait for a polite invitation to enter, which wasn't a surprise to Dan. He shook Angela's hand solemnly and strode into the house, saving a hostile look for Dan as he passed. Dan thought he even saw a gleam of disappointment in Pogo the dog's eyes.

Jeb sat on the sofa and folded his arms, Pogo alert at his feet.

"I'm sorry," Dan said. "Some things happened today and I forgot about the therapy appointment. Inexcusable."

Jeb said nothing, merely twitched a thick eyebrow.

"Um," Angela said. "I think maybe I'm responsible for the missed appointment. Dr. Blackwater was helping me."

"I appreciate you covering for him, missy," Jeb said, "but I've heard this tune before, many times."

Dan saw a glint of ire in Angela's eye. No matter what she'd been through, Angela Gallagher was a commissioned officer in the US Navy. He had a feeling Jeb was about to meet his match. "You may call me Angela," she said, "or Chaplain Gallagher, or even Captain, if you'd prefer."

Jeb's brows lifted in surprise. "Uh—"

She cut him off. "The doctor here might have been shirking his other appointments, but this time he has a valid reason. I was attacked this morning, and Dr. Blackwater rendered aid and assistance. That is the truth, whether you believe it or not."

Jeb blanched, and Dan almost laughed out loud. He felt a stir of pride for Angela standing ramrod straight, chin up, the determination making her impossibly gorgeous.

Gorgeous? He shut off the rampant thought.

Jeb cleared his throat. "Ah. Well, that puts a different spin on things. I apologize to both of you." Jeb gave her an appraising look. "Army?"

"Navy," Angela said, a degree of warmth creeping back into her voice.

"May I ask if you are all right, Chaplain?"

"Call me Angela, and, yes, thanks to Dan and my family, I wasn't badly hurt."

"I'm glad for that. I was a frontline medic during the Persian Gulf War. We appreciated our chaplains very much. I meant no disrespect."

She graced him with a smile. "And I served in Afghanistan, embedded with a marine unit. We appreciated our medics very much."

"Can't believe you were attacked here. What's going on in Cobalt Cove?"

"I'd love to know the answer to that one, too," Dan said.

"Was your attacker arrested?"

"No." She sat next to Jeb on the couch and stroked the dog's head. Pogo relaxed into a canine puddle of contentment.

"But he will be," Dan put in.

"Sweet dog," she said, smiling enough to show that enticing dimple.

"More than sweet," Jeb said. "She's a service dog. I came home from the war an emotional mess. Pogo keeps me centered, stays with me when I have panic attacks, nightmares. It's exponentially better now, but she's still there in case I need her."

Angela's face softened as she caressed the dog. "She can do all that?" she murmured.

"And more," Dan added. "I've seen her bring Jeb out of a flashback better than any therapist. Maybe a dog could help you, too," he blurted. Instantly he knew he'd gone too far.

Jeb shot him a questioning look. Of course she didn't want her PTSD discussed in front of a man she'd hardly met. *Way to go, Dr. Blackwater. Dolt.*

"You two have things to discuss. I'll be on my way." Bolting from the couch, she carried her coffee cup to the kitchen. "Thank you for the coffee."

He wished he could take back the words. Why couldn't he learn to keep his tongue still? His mother used to quote from Ecclesiastes, "Danny, the Lord says there's a 'time to be silent and a time to speak.'" Sadly, he had not mastered the former. He was the "foot in the mouth" champion, especially where women were concerned.

"Angela, please. Don't rush off. Marco and Donna are meeting us here shortly. It's starting to rain, anyway. You shouldn't walk with a storm coming in."

"I'll agree with that, Chaplain," Jeb said. "I've been a mean old bear, and I'd like a chance to show you my better side. I can do Dan's therapy right here, right now." He grinned and winked at her. "You can bar the door in case he tries to escape."

A small smile flicked across her face. "Well…"

"Anyway, Pogo likes the ladies. There aren't any coming around my place," Jeb said.

"Imagine that," Dan said.

Jeb grimaced as he got up. "Just for that, you get extra soft tissue work."

Angela took a position on the far end of the room, leaving as much space between them as she could. At least she hadn't left. Perhaps he could show his better side, too, the side that didn't butt into people's personal lives.

"So," Jeb said, as he began to flex and pull on Dan's fingers at the kitchen table. "Suppose you two tell me about your investigations."

"How did you know we were investigating anything?"

"I have an office at the hospital. Word traveled fast about the car explosion and Lila Brown. The police don't show up too often in this little town, and the walls have ears."

And Jeb had multiple sources from the gift shop girl to a cadre of janitors. The man was an incorrigible gossip. He knew who was expecting, dating, divorcing or struggling financially.

Dan followed Jeb's directions as he filled him in. "We're trying to figure out if a local named Tank Guzman had anything to do with Lila's accident. He says he's innocent and that Harry Gruber is trying to kill him for some reason which we haven't been able to ferret out."

Jeb frowned. "Is Guzman responsible for the attack on you, Angela?"

"I don't know," Angela said. "I couldn't see my attacker's face." Dan heard her suck in a breath. "The police seem to think it's got to be Tank, but I'm not convinced."

"What about Harry Gruber, Jeb? Do you know him?" Dan said.

"Gruber's a philanthropist, or he portrays himself to be. He's got a temper for sure. Back before he took over the clinic, I ran into him at the hospital. He got tired of waiting for an X-ray and raised such a fuss security asked him to leave."

"And his brother?"

"The dentist? Don't know much about him, but he drives a pretty beat-up car for a dentist. Rents a place in town, so his practice must not be all that lucrative."

"The police think the Grubers are completely innocent of any wrongdoing," Angela said with a touch of acid.

Jeb's eyes narrowed. "Torrey's running the investigation?"

"Yes."

"Huh." Jeb prodded him through another set of range-of-motion exercises.

"What?"

Jeb shrugged. "Probably nothing. I don't want to gossip."

"Since when?" Dan said.

Jeb had the decency to look chagrined. "I was enjoying a cup of coffee and a slice of apple pie at the Beachbum yesterday—"

"Aren't you supposed to be on a diet?" Dan said with a grin.

Jeb glared at him. "It was a very small piece, and anyway that's not the important part. While I was there, I just happened to notice Torrey having a meeting with someone. They were out back, though, not sitting at a table inside. I saw them through the window. I only made a mental note of it because Torrey was in street clothes and the two were heading toward the beach having a private talk. Neither were dressed for beachcombing if you see what I mean." Jeb sat back. "Excellent, Dr. Blackwater. Your tendon is fully repaired and rehabbed. You can return to your operating room without delay."

"Thanks, I'll start working on that," Dan said. "But who was Torrey meeting with?"

Angela moved closer, fully tuned in now, leaning forward to catch Jeb's reply. Her hair smelled like something fruity. Strawberry, or was it apple?

"Torrey was meeting with Gruber."

Angela groaned. "So Harry Gruber and Lieutenant Torrey are involved in this mess together?"

"Not Harry Gruber," Jeb said. "His brother, Peter."

Marco and Donna joined them shortly after Jeb packed up his kit and motored off with Pogo.

Dan called for one vegetarian pizza and another pepperoni, and set out a pitcher of ice water on the table. When they were munching thick slices of pizza, Marco delivered his news. "Ran some quick financials on Tank. His house is rented. Car is thirdhand. He was busted three years back for drug possession, and his mother paid the bail. He entered drug treatment. Busted again for a bar fight three months ago."

"I remember. I cleaned him up at the clinic. Lila and Peter fixed his broken tooth."

Donna wiped her chin with a napkin. "I took a look at Harry Gruber. He's squeaky clean. His wife died just before he moved to Cobalt Cove. He's got a divorced daughter and two grandchildren who live in San Diego. He's building a house there for them with an in-law unit where he can live. Sweet piece of oceanfront property. It's costing a chunk of change."

"How very domestic," Dan said. "No other issues?"

"Doesn't seem to be. Haven't looked at his brother yet, but I got a whiff that Peter's had some trouble with the ponies."

Donna wiped her mouth. "He's a gambler?"

"Is or was."

"Well, maybe you'd better move him up on the list," Dan said, repeating what he'd heard from Jeb.

Marco sat back in his chair. "So you think Torrey is compromised?"

"He is quick to defend the Grubers."

Marco frowned. "Nothing more dangerous than a dirty cop."

Rain battered against the windows. Angela walked over to watch the heaving ocean, and her sister joined her.

"Don't you want some pizza?" Donna asked.

"Not hungry," Angela said.

Donna reached out a hand but stopped short of touching her sister, and Angela felt a stab of pain. How distant they'd become since their teen days when they would fix each other's hair, believing the claim that one hundred brushstrokes was the optimal amount for the perfect healthy shine. So much laughter, so many whispered secrets, sister secrets that even her parents weren't privy to. Of all her siblings, she'd always been closest to Donna. The loss of that intimacy cut at her. There was fault on both sides, but since Donna had healed from her disastrous relationship and found Brent, she'd sought to repair the rift. Now the responsibility for their coolness toward each other lay squarely on Angela's shoulders.

It's not you, Donna, she wanted to say. *It's me.*

"Are you okay?" Donna asked in a whisper. "Today was horrible."

"I'm okay."

"Would you tell me if you weren't?"

"Probably not," she admitted with a smile.

Donna's face was grave. "Why not, Angie? We used to share everything. You know about the messes I've made, and you never judged me. Why won't you give me the chance to return that blessing?"

Angela reached up to finger her sister's mane of golden hair, the unruly strands that she'd endlessly braided in their teen years. "I just can't talk about things right now. I'm sorry."

Donna trapped Angela's fingers in her hands and squeezed hard. Angela felt a wave of fierce love, still there, still binding them together. She blinked against a wash of tears.

"I'm here anytime, Angie, and I love you. Brent and I are both praying for you."

She allowed an embrace, but Donna's hug was tentative, as if she knew Angela was as fragile as an eggshell for all her brave talk.

"Thank you," she said, grateful when her phone buzzed.

She clicked it on. "Hello?"

There was a scuffling noise, a moment of loud breathing, then a woman's voice. "Help me."

"Who is this?" she demanded.

"Cora Guzman," the woman said, half whispering. Angela hurried back to Marco and Dan, Donna following. She pressed the speakerphone button.

"I'm here with Dan and my family. What's wrong, Cora? Where are you?"

"Help me," she said. This time her voice came out in a hiss. "I'm supposed to meet him at the old lighthouse, but he's not here and I'm scared. My phone's almost dead."

"Who's supposed to meet you, Cora?"

"Tank. We're going to Mexico."

Running for their lives, Angela thought. *But why?*

"He was going to try one last time to convince her."

"Convince who?"

"I'm scared." Her voice broke. "I can see a car coming up the road. It's not Tank."

"I'll call the police, Cora," Angela said.

"They want us dead, too."

"The police? Why?" Angela wished she could see Cora's face. "Cora, you've got to tell us what's going on."

"I can't talk," Cora said. "They'll hear me. They're coming and the car's out of gas. I have to hide."

"Who, Cora? Who's coming?" Angela cried.

The line went dead.

against

him.

...as if all four of them came to the same conclusion at the same moment. Dan grabbed his rain jacket and tossed an extra one to Angela. Donna and Marco headed for the door.

Dan filled them in. "It's the lighthouse on the bluff. It's a ruin now, really, but the keeper's quarters are still standing and so is the tower, though it's wrecked."

"Should we call the police?" Donna said.

Dan considered Jeb's information about Torrey and Peter meeting outside the diner. All four of them exchanged a look.

"Torrey is a part of this somehow," Marco said. "I vote Dan and I check it out and let the women know if we need police involvement."

"Overruled, but thanks for sharing your idea,"

Donna said cheerfully as she and Angela pulled on their coats.

"But—" Marco started.

"We'll be careful," Angela said. "I'm not going to let anybody sneak up on me a second time."

"I'll be your point man," Dan said, guiding Angela to his truck. "Meet you there," he called to Marco and Donna.

"Nobody makes a move until we're all four in position," Marco said.

"We've got to hurry," Angela said.

They ran into the driving rain, and in moments they were on the road, Dan's truck in the lead.

He took the road out of town as quickly as conditions would allow, his mind racing. "He said Tank went to try one last time to convince her."

Angela frowned. "Her meaning Lila? That explains why he was on his way to her house when we surprised him."

"But convince her of what? Does she have some evidence about the Grubers? About Peter maybe? She works with him—maybe she knows something."

She worried her lower lip between her teeth.

At the top of the bluff, a bolt of lightning ripped through the sky, illuminating the remains of what had once been a grand lighthouse. He'd spent some time hiking the area, photographing the square wooden tower with the attached keeper's dwelling. The whole structure had been built of wood and stone in 1879 and had served valiantly until the weather and technology had rendered its grand catoptric light obsolete. He'd heard some investor had bought the place twenty years ago with the intent to restore it. Now it was too late; the old lighthouse was beyond any hope of resurrection.

He turned the wipers on high and shot a glance at Angela. "You up for this?"

She paused before answering. "To be honest, I feel like running away."

"You don't have—"

"But I'm in," she said firmly. "Cora needs us, and I'm not going to let my fear get in the way of helping her."

"You were attacked today."

"I was attacked a long time ago," Angela said. "Nothing can be any worse than that." The wipers sloshed against the window, the rain falling in sheets now.

Was it a time for silence or speech? He was struggling through it when she spoke.

"Cora is Julio's sister-in-law. He would want her and his brother taken care of."

"But he would not want you to risk yourself. His whole purpose in Afghanistan as chaplain's assistant was to keep you safe. He'd want the same for you now."

Her voice was hard, edged with despair. "Julio gave away his life for mine. I've got to make it mean something, even if I can't minister anymore.

I've got to do that at least." She turned gleaming eyes on his. "Please tell me you understand, Dan. Nobody else can because they weren't there. Tell me you understand, even if you don't agree."

Without a word, he reached over and took her hand, caressing the long elegant fingers in his. "I do. Completely. You're a strong person, Angela."

"No," she whispered. "I'm a weak person who's trying to show up instead of run away."

He grazed her knuckles with his lips thinking he had never seen greater courage even in the most decorated soldiers he'd had the privilege to meet. Battle-hardened men with multiple tours faced their missions with the same incredible spirit of self-sacrifice. His breathing shallowed out.

Your life does mean something, especially to me.

And what did she mean to him exactly? Friendship? Something more? His brain tried to put words to the feeling. Just a bond formed long ago amid the desolation of war. The one thing he'd learned at Kandahar, was the profound connection of those who had served each other. It was a blood bond, one of the finest qualities a human could possess, a pale reflection of God's commitment to the people He loved.

I'm going to keep you safe, Angela.

He looked out into the raging storm.

And no one on earth is going to get in my way.

Pressing the gas, he pushed faster as they took the remainder of the rocky slope up to the lighthouse.

* * *

Puddled water splashed up, soaking Angela's socks and shoes as she got out of the truck. She stepped around the no-trespassing sign the police had tacked to a metal pole. The ground was littered with broken bottles, and the swirl of graffiti on the nearby rock pile indicated they had not been successful. Marco handed her a flashlight.

Allowing her eyes to adjust to the darkness, she strained to make out any signs of Cora or her pursuer.

"There," Marco said, pointing.

The next sizzle of lightning revealed an older-model Ford, the rear bumper protruding from behind the corner of the keeper's quarters. There was no sign of another vehicle.

Her heart thumped.

They approached quietly, Dan edging around to the driver's side, Marco opposite.

Angela saw with a thrill of dread that the driver's door was open, keys still pinging in the ignition. Marco slid open the passenger door and checked the glove box. "It's registered to Tank Guzman," he whispered.

Cora, where are you?

There was no indication of which direction she might have taken.

"Going to check out the tower," Marco said, voice low.

"I'll come," Donna mouthed.

Dan nodded. "We'll search the keeper's quarters."

Angela fell in behind him. The rain trickled down her collar, chilling her spine and soaking the bandage on her back. Since water blew under her hood, her hair was soon plastered to her skull. They picked their way over rocks and planks of rotted wood that had fallen long ago as the building descended into decay. The ground was slick, and Dan offered his hand, which she gripped tight.

Stumbling as they went, she looked at the shrubs, dark branches waving in the violent wind. Where had Cora hidden? Or had she been found? Abducted? Killed? Angela suppressed a shiver.

The dilapidated structure affixed to the wall of the four-sided tower had a large door, bookended on each side by two rectangular windows. The glass had long since been broken away, leaving three gaping black mouths, frozen in a silent scream. The scent of the sea mingled with the smell of rotting wood, mold and something else she could not identify.

Dan stepped inside first, blocking her from following until he'd beamed his light around.

"Clear," he whispered back at her. "See if you can spot anything."

She entered, almost overwhelmed by the black emptiness, the smell of decay. She'd seen such barren spaces before, prayed in them, the bombed-out homes where lives had ended, dreams had died. But she'd had God right by her side in those moments, to offer hope to the hopeless and the confidence that there was life in Him, a future in the face of gut-wrenching pain.

God, where are You? she thought as the memories of the past mingled with the awful blackness of the present. She could see nothing but the wind-blown trash that had accumulated inside, shards of broken glass catching her flashlight beam.

Nothing.

There had been no word from Marco and Donna, and clearly Cora had not driven away. A bit of color caught her attention, and she bent down. It was a tube of lip balm, berry flavored. It was not surprising to find such an item in the detritus, but the fact that it was clean indicated it had been dropped recently. Very recently. As someone fumbled in their bag?

She held it up. "Cora was here."

He nodded slowly, eyes scanning.

She followed Dan's gaze. The beach? The lighthouse occupied a square lot on a rock cliff that jutted out over the ocean. There was a sharply plunging descent down to a curve of beach not twenty feet from their current location. Would she have headed there? It made no sense, but then Cora had been terrified and might have fled without thinking it through.

Dan checked his watch. "High tide soon."

Which meant that the little beach would be submerged. And Cora with it? She swallowed.

They exited the keeper's quarters. A flicker of light from the wooden tower indicated Marco and Donna were continuing their search. They had almost reached the lantern room, hemmed in by the rusty iron railing. Dan sent Marco a text.

"Not sure he's getting them," Dan said.

"Be careful, you two," she breathed. Those ruined stones, the rusted railings and rain pouring through the holes in the fractured walls. *Marco will keep Donna safe*, she reminded herself. *If she lets him*, her mind added ruefully.

Dan and Angela took the torturously steep stone stairs that had been hewn out of the side of the rocky cliff. Pooled water made every step treacherous, and the journey was slow. Dan slipped, nearly catapulting down the stairs, but Angela was able to grab the back of his jacket and anchor him while he regained his balance.

"Thanks," he whispered.

"Anytime."

At the bottom, they stepped into ankle-deep water. Dan checked his cell and found they had no signal there. The tide had already pulled the waves up and over the shallow lip of beach. How much longer did they have before they would have to escape back up the steps? She wanted to ask Dan, but he suddenly jerked her into the shadows, behind a jag of rock.

"I heard something," he mouthed in her ear. "Going to check it out."

"Me, too," she said.

"No. Water's rising fast. Go back to the stairs and call Marco. You can get a signal there and we need to be sure he knows where we are."

"Dan—"

"Just call. Better four of us knowing the situation than one obnoxious doctor."

"And a waterlogged chaplain," she finished. She'd surprised herself. Did she actually still believe she was a chaplain?

His face lit with a smile, and he pressed a quick kiss to her cheek. She gasped.

"Sorry," he said, brushing a strand of soaked hair back from her eyes. "I've got a thing for dimples." He leaned in again, his mouth so close to hers. Tingles coursed through her nerves, but he stopped and pressed his cheek to her forehead. "Go now, Angela," he said, grazing a finger over her chin as he pulled away.

Her cheek warmed where he'd kissed her, the only spot in her body that seemed to feel any heat whatsoever. She slogged back to the stairs. It took her five steps up before she got a signal. "Marco, we're down here. On the beach. Dan's heard something."

"On it."

His response relieved her. At least she knew they were safe. She pocketed the phone and made her slippery way back down the stairs, once again splashing into the frigid water which was now at mid-shin level. A rumble of thunder made her jump. She could not see any sign of Dan thanks to the fin of rock that blocked her view.

She longed to creep around that barrier, but she knew the smart thing to do would be to stay put and wait for Marco and Donna. A shout rose above the pounding waves; there was no mistaking it.

She edged out a few steps, trying to peer around the rock.

To her left she saw Marco and Donna begin their journey down the steps. They would arrive in moments, and she could wait no longer. Dan needed her help. She could feel it.

With the sharp rocks cutting at her hands, she sloshed her way gingerly around the protruding section of cliff, the water now climbing to her knees. Shivering, muscles rigid, she pressed on. Darkness seemed like a smothering blanket, with only glimpses of weak moonlight penetrating the clouds.

Inch by inch, she cleared the rocks, finding herself in a bowl-shaped cove where the cliff wall was more gently sloped. A crescent of rocky beach still showed, but not for long, she reckoned. Straining her eyes, she sought any sign of Dan. The light was pinched off by drifting clouds. Now she was in complete darkness, water slapping around her thighs as her legs slowly went numb. She did not want to activate her flashlight for fear it would give away her location to Cora's pursuer, but the minutes stretched by and there was no sound from Dan.

She had only a few more minutes before she would need to return to the steps or be totally submerged. After a deep breath, she flicked on the flashlight.

The beam caught Dan in the water, apparently shouting at two figures on the cliff side, though she could not make out his words.

He shot a surprised look at Angela, took a reflexive step toward her. There was a scream from above, and one of the figures lost their grip on the rocks and tumbled backward into the ocean.

FOURTEEN

Dan lunged into the surf. Salt water stung his eyes as he frantically tried to locate the fallen victim. Angela headed right for the spot, her flashlight beaming a path for him to follow. Splashing awkwardly, he surged against the agitation of the waves toward Angela.

"Here," she yelled, groping around in the water.

He churned to her side, grabbed the back of a soggy shirt and hauled with all his strength.

A face emerged, dazed and sputtering.

"Tank," Angela said, shocked. "What happened?"

Dan pointed to the cliff where the other figure struggled upward, face nothing more than a streak of white in the darkness. "That's Cora. Tank was climbing up behind her."

"I got to get her away, somewhere safe," Tank moaned.

There was a scream from above, and a cascade of rock broke loose from the cliff side. Dan's stomach twisted. A fall down those rocks from that height would batter her to pieces. Cora had somehow managed to hold on, at least for the moment. No telling how long that would last until the cold and fear overwhelmed her.

Marco and Donna splashed over.

Marco took in Cora's progress. "Got any rope in your truck?"

Dan nodded.

"I'll get it. Lower it to her."

"I'll climb up from here and get her harnessed," Dan said.

"No," Angela blurted. "That's too dangerous."

"I'm a pretty good rock climber, among other things."

Marco cocked his head. "You sure, Doc?"

"I'm always sure," Dan said. "That's part of my charm." He pushed Tank toward them. "Take him back up the stairs before the tide gets any higher."

Marco grabbed one of Tank's arms and Donna the other.

"I don't think this is smart," Angela said.

He chuckled. "I'm sure Jeb would agree," he said, heading toward the cliff. "Stay with Tank. Call for an ambulance."

"Dan…" she started.

He looked over, framed from behind by a wash of rolling waves, tall and strong even against the storm.

What could she say? *Be careful? I care about you?*

Did she care? Could she possibly have feelings for a man at this time in her life? She stood frozen, mute, as the water rose and slapped around her legs. Donna moved toward the stairs with Marco.

Dan came close and put his hands on either side of her face.

"Hey, Chaplain," he said. "Tank needs you. Go do your thing."

"I can't just leave you here."

He ducked to look right in her face, his eyes capturing hers. "All you have to do is get him up those stairs. One foot in front of the other."

One foot in front of the other seemed impossible if it meant leaving him alone, at the mercy of the ocean. Then his lips were on her temple, and he kissed her there.

"Time to go." He stepped back and gave her a cocky thumbs-up. Donna tugged on her jacket sleeve.

"Let's go, Angela. We need your help. Dan will be okay."

Her body felt leaden with fear and cold as she half walked, half swam back to the stone steps. The rising water was waist high, breaking with slaps of jarring cold against her numbed body. Shuddering now, she felt the bite of the wind, and each movement was an excruciating effort. What if Dan did not come back? He was a doctor, not a special forces operative or a firefighter, skilled in cliff rescue.

Lord... Panic immediately overwhelmed the prayer.

One foot in front of the other. She focused on her feet, plowing through, pushing on though her body screamed for her to stop.

Marco and Donna hauled Tank up one step at a time, their progress too slow.

"You two need to take him," Marco said. "I've got to get that rope down to Cora before she falls."

Donna nodded, taking up position at one of Tank's shoulders, and Angela stepped up to support the other. Tank was able to help a little as they struggled up step after step. She looked down at the stone, black and unforgiving as they inched their way up. Angela's muscles were screaming and her breath came in frantic puffs as they finally crested the top.

"Dan's truck," Donna said. "It will give Tank some protection from the rain." With backbreaking effort, they dragged Tank to the truck, propping him in the passenger side. Donna found a blanket behind the seat and wrapped it around him as best she could.

He blinked, as if he was coming out of a trance. "Cora. Where is she?"

"They're getting her," Angela said, forcing the words through her stiff, frozen lips.

He nodded, and his eyes focused on hers. Teeth

chattering, lips nearly blue, he clutched the blanket to himself. "I…I," he stammered, then stopped, hands falling slack, face twisting with emotion.

Angela pulled up the edge of the blanket, tucking it around his shoulders. "It's okay. You don't have to talk now."

Donna whispered in Angela's ear. "This has turned into a full-blown rescue. I'm going to call the police if they haven't already been notified. We don't have a choice."

Angela nodded as her sister stepped away.

Tank coughed. "We were going to run. He found out about our meeting place somehow. He must have bugged my phone. Why didn't I think of that?"

A bout of violent shivering cut off his words. Angela wished she had the keys to the truck so she could turn on the heater.

He coughed until he choked for air. "I was waiting in the lighthouse, and I saw a car come. I ran to help Cora. We thought we could hide on the beach, but the tide was coming in."

Rain slammed against the windshield, thunder crashing so loud it shook the ground under her feet.

"I have to go help," she said. "You can tell me the rest later."

He reached out a hand, his cold fingers clawing at hers. "Thank you…for coming for her. I'm sorry."

Angela felt stricken. She had come, but had it been too late? Cora had looked so small, barely a dot against the cruel expanse of rock. She squeezed his hand and pulled away, a tiny piece of her wondering.

I'm sorry. For involving Angela in the first place? For attacking her?

What if she was wrong about Gruber being the one?

But Tank couldn't be her attacker. Could he? A man who loved his wife? Loved his brother? And hated her for causing his brother's death. The whole situation was a nightmare. "I've got to go help."

"Wait." Tank rooted under the blanket and reached into his jacket. He pulled out a capped plastic cylinder, the type of canister that used to hold film back before the digital revolution. "In here, in case I don't make it. You can get him."

"What are you saying, Tank?" She wanted to press more, but she heard voices shouting over the howling wind.

"Go," he said. "Go help my wife."

She stowed the canister in the pocket of her jeans and followed her sister along the cliffs.

The wind roared, blowing the rain into stinging needles.

They found Marco attaching the rope to a sturdy iron pole wedged into the rock. He tied a knot in the other end and began to feed it over the lip of cliff. When he'd fed out fifty feet or so, he approached the edge.

"Rope's away," he shouted down to Dan. "Got it?"

It seemed like an interminable length of time, and then the faint shout of Dan's reply came.

Angela went weak with relief.

"He's got it. Tying her in," Marco said.

Another few minutes of anxious waiting, and they heard Dan's signal. The three of them hauled on the rope. In the distance, a siren wailed. Angela hoped it was the ambulance. No telling what Cora's condition was. Or Dan's.

She pulled harder, the rough rope digging into her palms. Hand over hand they toiled until her skin was burning, eyes nearly blinded by the downpour.

Finally, through the deluge, Cora appeared, face contorted and scraped.

Angela and Donna ran to her and eased her over. While Marco sent the rope back down for Dan, they carried Cora to the truck and put her next to Tank. His face quivered with naked relief. He pulled her to him, wrapping the blanket around her and speaking softly in Spanish, lips pressed to her wet hair. She was shivering, crying, babbling.

"Cora," he said. "I'm so sorry. It's my fault. All of it. I'm going to get you out of this mess—I promise."

Angela sighed as she saw Dan climbing over the cliff edge, Marco holding firmly on to his arm. The relief overcame the cold and the pain in her back and hands.

One foot in front of the other, inch by painful

inch, the four of them had conquered the storm and the sea and brought Tank and Cora to safety.

And Dan. He stood slightly bent over, hands on hips, struggling to catch his breath. She wanted to run to him, throw her arms around him and send up a prayer of jubilant thanksgiving.

The next moment seemed to unroll in slow motion. She smiled at him, her arm half lifted in a greeting. She took two steps toward him.

Then a shot rang out.

And then another.

Dan dove for the ground, Marco right behind him. The shots came from somewhere in the trees, bullets sparking where they hit rock.

"Get down, get down," he yelled at the women.

Through the driving rain he could not see where Donna and Angela had gone. Another shot drilled into the side of Marco's rental car. The ambulance, lights flashing, pulled up and rolled to a stop.

Marco tried to shout a warning, but the paramedic was already on his way out, carrying his kit, oblivious to the danger. A shot exploded the light bar on the top of the rig. The medic dove back inside, no doubt radioing for the police.

The shooter seemed to be bent on creating chaos, or he was an unskilled marksman. Another bullet hit the iron pole, ricocheting with a shower of sparks.

"The women," Dan shouted. He could find no sign of them in the inky darkness.

"Near your truck," Marco called back. "Tank and Cora are inside, so they've got cover."

Dan knew he had to get to Angela and Donna. They might be lying unprotected from the bullets flying around them. He was not sure if Angela would have the ability to take proper cover, or if the shots would bring her PTSD roaring to life. He'd been so sure, sending her up those stairs with Marco and Donna.

One foot at a time, right into the range of a shooter. His gut clamped down tight.

"Go on three," Marco shouted. "I'll draw his fire."

Dan did a slow count to three and then beelined it for the truck as Marco leaped from his position. Dan's feet pounded over the rubble. Marco ran out into the open toward the trees for several yards before he dove behind a pile of rotting wood.

Get to Angela. The thought throbbed relentlessly through his mind as he sprinted, ignoring the fact that a bullet might punch through his skull at any moment. Slipping and sliding, he tried desperately to keep his balance. Three yards left. He could see no movement from inside the vehicle. Were Angela and Donna underneath? Had they piled into the cab to seek protection?

Dan was inches from the truck when the engine throbbed to life. How was that possible since he had the keys in his pocket? As he struggled to catch up, the truck jerked forward. Dan sprinted closer, got a hand around the back bumper. It jerked forward out of his grasp, careened around the ambulance and up the slope to the main road. Dan pursued for a few minutes until he stumbled and fell.

The truck must have distracted the shooter, who fired once in the direction of the vanishing vehicle.

One more bullet, probably intended to hit the truck, slammed into the side of the lighthouse, so close to Dan's head that he heard it whistle by, felt the flying chips of wood on his cheek. Once again he hit the ground.

Gasping for breath, heart slamming into his ribs, he peered through the curtains of falling rain. No more shots. To his right, the medics still crouched in their vehicle. In the distance, the sound of police sirens. Past the lighthouse, Marco cautiously peered around his shelter, checking to see if the shooter was finished.

His mind took in all the details simultaneously, but his gut flared with an unbearable question.

What had happened to Angela and her sister?

"Angela," he called out, voice low.

No answer. No shots. Silence.

"Angela," he said, voice rising until it rang out in a shout. "Answer me."

FIFTEEN

Angela's fear choked off her breath as she looked up from the ditch behind the lighthouse into which she and her sister had dived. She kept her eyes pressed tightly shut. What would she find when she opened them? Not death, surely not that. Her sister, lying next to her, lifeless and silent. Like Julio. Horror kept her eyes shut, her body paralyzed.

"Donna," she whispered. "Donna."

And then in an answer to a prayer she had not been able to utter, she felt Donna's hand squeeze hers.

"Here."

They sat up, amid the rock and debris. Angela clutched her sister, crying.

"I thought…"

Donna shook her head, fingers laced tightly in Angela's. "I'm okay. You, too?"

She nodded.

Dan's voice cut through the night, shouting now.

"Angela? Donna?" he roared.

"Here," Donna called, when Angela could not manage a response.

Marco and Dan made it to their location in seconds. Dan's face was stricken as he wrapped Angela in a hug. "I couldn't find you. Are you both okay? Is anyone hurt?"

"Not hurt." Angela continued to work on getting her breathing under control. "We took cover here. What about you?"

"We're okay," Marco said.

Dan nodded. "Fortunately, we're faster than we look."

She could not see much in the dark but the feel of Dan's arms was strong and sure, heart beating steadily in his chest as he pressed her to him.

"Is the shooter gone?" Donna said.

Marco nodded. "Saw him take off up the trail. Tank hot-wired the truck. Might be able to catch them in the rental. I'll go."

"No you won't," Donna said, pointing to the police car that was careening down the trail. It screeched to a stop, and Torrey and another office leaped out. Torrey approached them while his partner spoke to the paramedics, who were just venturing out of their vehicle. Dan let her go, somewhat reluctantly she thought.

"Talk to me," Torrey said.

They gave him a quick rundown. Torrey scowled. "Where did Tank take your truck?"

"I don't know," Dan said with a shrug. "We were

too busy dodging bullets to ask him. Shouldn't you be more concerned about the shooter?"

"I'll ask Tank about that myself when I get my hands on him."

"You can't blame this on Tank" Angela said. "We were shot at, all of us."

Fury shone on Torrey's face clearly through the rain. "I don't believe one single word out of Tank's mouth. If he was honest, he'd talk to us. I'm tired of this game. I'm going to find him and he's going to come clean."

"Someone is shooting at him and his wife. He's scared."

Torrey's eyes gleamed cold in the moonlight. "He should be."

A shiver ran up Angela's spine.

Dan noticed Angela shudder. He wiped his eyes. "We need to get these ladies out of this storm. We're going now. You know where to find us."

Torrey did not argue. He moved away, training his flashlight over the ground where the truck had left deep grooves as Tank made his escape.

They loaded up into Marco's car. Angela looked dangerously weary. He wanted to wrap her up in another tight hug, press away the cold and reassure her. They were safe. She was safe. He sat in the passenger seat and cranked the heater. Angela had her arm around her sister's shoulders, and the two were huddled together. The sight was comforting to him. *Find your way back to the people who love you, Angela.*

Love you? Something about the word made his heart skip. Not love. Not from him. Love was something that he could not imagine for himself anymore, since AnnaLisa left him. He did not have space for it inside, or perhaps he did not want to make space for it. Love was too flimsy, too fragile, too easily lost, like the patients he'd tended. Fragile, fleeting, gone.

"Down there," Marco said, stopping the car abruptly and jerking Dan from his thoughts.

Dan would have missed it, but a trail of broken branches pointed the way to his truck. It stood, doors open, lights off, windshield wipers slapping.

They approached warily, Marco edging up the driver's side. "All clear," he said after a moment.

The truck was abandoned. A bullet hole had punched through the side window, sending cracks splintering through the glass. Dan checked for blood and found none.

"Why'd he stop here?" Donna said. "Why not drive the truck to the airport if that's where they were headed?"

"He's scared," Marco said. "Shooter knows his plans, knows he's in Dan's truck. Gonna run on foot. Get out of town as quick as he can."

They got back in the car, and Marco phoned Torrey to report the truck's location.

Angela had scooted over to the far side of the

seat, staring out the window, hands clenched tightly in her lap. "What is happening here?" she whispered after they took off again.

"What, Angie?" Donna said.

Dan didn't like the strained quality to her voice. "This is supposed to be safe."

"What is?" her sister pressed.

"Being back in the States, in California. We're not in a war zone here." Her voice was tense, high pitched. "But we've been shot at, attacked. Tank is running for his life. How is that safety? Is this what we're meant to come home to?"

Donna reached for her hand, but Angela snatched it away.

Marco's jaw tensed, but he kept his eyes on the road. "It isn't," he said. "Time to go home to Coronado. Forget this case. Forget Tank."

"How can I forget him?" Angela said. "How can I leave him to die like his brother?"

"He's gotten himself into trouble by his own choices. None of that has anything to do with you." Marco darted a quick look in the rearview mirror.

Angela exhaled heavily. "Who will tell his mother she's lost both her sons?"

"It might not come to that. Anyway, you don't have to be involved," Dan said. "We can find someone else to work the case."

Marco nodded. "I'll stay. You go home with Donna. He's right. Doesn't have to be you."

"Yes," she said, pinning him with a gaze so anguished it cut at him. "It does have to be me. I asked God a long time ago to send me to do His will."

"Maybe this isn't—" Donna said.

"Yes, it is," she hissed. "He linked me with the Guzman family for some reason. I watched Julio die, and God let me live."

"He didn't spare you so you could sacrifice yourself for Tank," Dan said sharply.

"I don't know why He spared me," she cried. "So I could continue to minister? Well, I can't. I'm not able to be a chaplain, not anymore." Angela's voice dropped. "I need to try and save Tank. That's all I can do."

"But what if you can't?" Donna said, jaw taut. "What if this is too much for you?"

"It's not," she said.

"Angie—"

"I said, it's not." As if struck by a sudden thought, she patted her pocket and pulled out a film canister. "Here. Look at this. He told me this will help."

"What is it?"

She opened the canister and unfurled a piece of paper, mercifully spared from the rain.

"It's names. Three names. Betty Hernandez, Ralph Pickford, Oliver Clark." She read it again, fingers tracing the tiny print.

Dan let the names ring through his memory. Something dark and colder than the storm-washed air sank down on him.

"You know them, Dan?" Angela was saying.

"Just one of them. Ralph Pickford. He's a drifter. I've treated him at the clinic, and so has Lila. We did a veterans event where we provided free physicals and dental exams, haircuts, the whole nine yards. It was about six months ago."

"Have you seen him recently?"

"Yes," he said, heart thudding loud in his ears. "That's the funny thing."

"Where?"

"At the hospital, the day Lila bolted. I saw him in an exam room waiting for the doctor."

"What doctor?"

"Patricia Lane."

The wipers continued to thwack, struggling to keep up with the torrents of rain.

"I'll go talk to her tomorrow," Dan said.

Marco made the final turn into town and dropped Dan off at his house. He shot another look at Angela before he got out. He offered a smile, which she returned halfheartedly.

"We'll talk later, okay?" he said.

"There's another place we should go." Her face was haunted. "Another lead we should follow."

He had a feeling he knew what she was about to say. "Marco and Donna can do it."

"No. Tank might have told his mother where he was headed. We…I have to talk to Mrs. Guzman."

"I don't think that's a good idea," he said softly. Her eyes blazed, reflecting metallic moonlight back at him. "Stop telling me what I should and shouldn't do."

"Someone has to rein you in," he snapped.

"You're not my doctor, and I don't have to take advice from you."

His blood pulsed hot. "Maybe it's about time you did take some advice. We're not exactly in a safe situation here."

"I know that. I heard the shots, too." She set her mouth in a thin line.

"Then quit being so stubborn."

"Is that an order?" she shot back.

Marco shifted on the seat. "It's late. Leave the topic open for now. Donna and I will chase down the other two names on Tank's list—see if we can tie them to the Grubers. Keep the channels open. Everybody knows what everybody's doing. No one heads out alone—understood?"

Though Dan bridled at being given orders on top of being told off by Angela, he knew Marco was right.

He agreed, stepping away from the car and watching it head back toward the hotel.

Patricia Lane was a competent doctor.

Lila Brown worked at Gruber's clinic.

Ralph Pickford was a patient at both the hospital and the clinic. Could he be the link that might shed some light on who wanted Tank dead and was willing to stage a shoot-up to keep them from finding him?

Standing in the rain was getting him nowhere but on his way to freezing, so he headed inside. From underneath the shelter he'd built for Babs, the cat meowed pitifully.

"I don't want a pet," he said. "You're safe and dry in there."

The cat mewed again, piteously.

"It's not like you belong to me—you just sort of showed up here."

He could see Bab's whiskers trembling in the wind, drops of rain quivering there like crystal notes on a music staff.

With a sigh he opened the door. "All right. Get inside, why don't you?" He waited until the cat shot past him, streaking under the sofa.

Another crack of thunder rumbled through the sky. It made him think of rifle fire. He hoped it did not awaken any flashbacks for Angela.

"Might as well make yourself at home, Babs."

At least one female had the good sense to follow the doctor's orders.

Donna insisted Angela take the first shower. It was bliss to feel the hot water chasing the cold from her body, but Angela could not shake the chill of fear from her insides. Tank had been petrified; Cora, too. Her own emotions had run the gamut from terror for her own life to anger at Dan for doing nothing more than trying to keep her safe.

She felt like a pinball, shooting haphazardly from one emotion to the next.

She climbed under the covers and clasped her hands tight. She wanted to pour her prayers out to God, to entreat Him to let her find Tank and bring him to safety, to ground her back in His love and peace. But when she closed her eyes she could not stop the images pouring through her mind. Julio's smiling face, his rich laughter, the pop of gunfire, her own screams, the beginning of the darkness.

She felt Donna lie on the bed next to her and slowly reached out a hand to touch her sister.

"Praying?" Donna murmured.

"Every time I try…" Her throat choked off the words. She wished her sister would move away, leave her to the misery that would not let go, but Donna did not. Instead she curled up next to Angela and began to trace circles onto her back, the way they had when they were children.

Something is wrong with me, she wanted to blurt out. *I'm lost.* But nothing came out, nothing at all.

Her sister murmured, soft and low, "When I messed up my life, Angie, I didn't think God was listening anymore."

Angela knew. Donna had taken up with the wrong man who had nearly gotten her killed. She'd walked away from the Gallaghers, especially their father, whose advice Donna could not abide.

"After Nate, all I felt was a massive void, separation from Him and my family, everybody," Donna said. "I didn't want to be around Him or any of you, remember?"

"Yes."

"I was horrible, lashing out, trying to punish you all for my own failures. And do you remember what you said to me in the hospital when I woke up with a broken back and I thought I'd never walk again?"

She shook her head.

"You came to pray with me, and I screamed at you to get out and take your prayers and petitions with you."

It had been just before Angela deployed to Afghanistan. She remembered the rage in Donna's eyes, rage that did not quite cover up the intense fear.

Donna sighed. "You waited until I stopped yelling and you looked at me with love and compassion and you said, 'Donna, God hasn't left you. You're still connected to Him. And if you can't pray right now, that's okay. I'm going to do it for you.'"

Angela closed her eyes. How sure she'd been, how convinced of her own ability to counsel, to help people find peace. "That seems like a lifetime ago," she whispered.

Donna traced more circles of comfort onto Angela's back. "So now I'm returning the favor. I'm going to pray for you, Angie, because you can't do it for yourself right now and someday soon you're going to feel that connection again. Until then, God packed your life full of people who will hold you up when you can't do it yourself."

Packed with people. Her mother, Donna, Candace, Sarah.

Dan? All precious comforts, but there was only one relationship that would restore her fully. She could not speak. If only she could again feel the Father's love, His grace moving through her. She stayed silent as her sister prayed over her, pouring out all the entreaties that she could not utter for herself. When Donna finished, she gave her sister a kiss, pulled up the covers and climbed into her own bed.

Thank you, Angela wanted to say. The prayer had not blasted away the darkness, but one tiny corner of the gloom lightened a fraction, as if there could be a chance, the slimmest hope, that morning might come.

Her phone buzzed with a text. She read the screen.

I'm sorry for being bossy. Wanted to say I'm praying for you. D

Praying for you. Her sister. And Dan, the branches that might just hold her up until she could rediscover that precious connection to the vine.

She pressed her hands together again, held on to that fragile feeling and drifted off to sleep.

* * *

The next morning she knocked on Dan's front door, allowing her body to take action in spite of good sense. He'd been trying to help last night, and she'd struck out at him like a disgruntled snake. She sucked in a deep breath. New beginning. The coastal air was crisp, rain washed; chunks of driftwood and kelp had been tossed onto the sand from the previous night's storm. Dan appeared at the door, hair tousled, barefoot, wearing gray sweatpants and a T-shirt. He squinted, one eye closed, rubbing his stubbled chin as if he thought he was hallucinating.

"Angela?"

She held up a white paper bag and a cardboard tray with two cups of coffee. "My turn to bring breakfast."

He stood there, staring.

"To quote someone else I know, the coffee is hot. Are you going to let me in?"

He jerked into action, shoving the door open and ushering her inside. "I didn't expect to see you so early. I figured you'd be sleeping in. How are you feeling?"

"Better than last night. I walked over while Marco was out running."

He frowned.

"There were plenty of people out and about, and Donna texted me every block it seemed like."

"Did you get some sleep last night?"

"Not really, but…" She shrugged. "I appreciated your text, especially after I snapped at you."

He smiled. "It's true. I've been praying for you since the day you rolled into town, and you snapped at me then, too."

She thrust a cup of coffee into his hand, cheeks warm. "Thank you. I wanted to reassure you that I'm okay. I can do what I need to do today."

He watched her, gray eyes thoughtful. "It would be fine if you weren't."

"But I am," she insisted. "I'm ready to go talk to Dr. Lane and ask her about Ralph Pickford…and visit Mrs. Guzman," she said, though her mouth had suddenly gone dry.

He sipped some coffee. "All right. Can I have five minutes to shower and shave so I don't scare anyone?"

"Sure."

"What's in the bag?"

"Donuts, but now you only have four minutes and fifty-five seconds."

"Man," he said. "And you say I'm bossy."

He hustled off to the back of the house. She contented herself sipping coffee and watching a cat stalking a leaf under the couch. Surprising. She hadn't figured him the pet-owner type. On the wall there were pictures of Dan on his graduation from medical school, one of him posing on a sailboat with a friend. On a shelf, on top of some neatly stacked medical journals, was a box with his medical bag inside.

When he emerged in jeans and a soft T-shirt that brought out the silver in his eyes she gestured to the box.

"Are you getting ready to go back to your hospital job?"

He shrugged. "Not yet."

"Why not?"

He accepted the bag she offered and took a bite of a sugar donut. "Been nursing the hand back to full force."

"Jeb seems to think you're ready for action."

"Maybe."

She noted the hesitation, so uncharacteristic for this self-assured surgeon. She wanted to understand. "Does it have something to do with what you said earlier, that you came back from the war a different man?"

He raised his chin. "Don't know."

"If anybody can understand, it's me."

"Like I said, I don't know that I have to explain it to you. Do I?"

Did he? Yet he continually expected her to discuss her situation, even in front of his physical therapist. Her blood warmed. "No, but you're telling me a lot that I should get help, and it's okay not to be all right. Is that just something you say to other people but it doesn't apply to you?"

The silver flashed to gray. "We're not in the same situation."

"Maybe we have more in common than you want to admit."

"You don't know me as well as you think."

"Maybe I do. You're happy to see the problems in me but not in yourself. Is that an occupational hazard for a doctor?"

"No more than it is for chaplains."

She pursed her lips. "I'm clear on my own problems, Dr. Blackwater. Are you clear on yours?"

He stared at her. "Did you come here to pick a fight?"

"No, I guess I just got tired of being the only one who is expected to share my troubles."

"You don't share them," he said flatly. "You try to hide them."

"And you don't?"

"No, I don't. I hurt my hand and stepped away from my practice. That's all."

She tamped down on the anger kindling in her belly. "Let's drop it. We've got a job to do, so why don't we get started?"

"Excellent idea. We'll have to take my convertible since the police still have my truck."

Great, she thought. What had started out as a nice gesture had turned into accusations and harsh words. Now she would be in even closer proximity to the man who made her feelings tangle up like seaweed in a storm. Was Dan really hiding from his own struggles, or did it make her feel better to think he was not as together as he seemed?

The confusion left her nerves twitching.

Just get this case solved, she told herself. *And then you don't have to face Dan Blackwater again.*

SIXTEEN

Dan fumed on the way to the hospital. Angela Gallagher was in no position to be accusing him of hiding from his problems. His choice not to return to surgery wasn't because of lingering impact from his past. He'd chosen to do other things, to give himself a break.

A break that had lasted far longer than he'd intended, hand injury notwithstanding.

"What are you hiding from? We haven't been out on a date all week," he remembered AnnaLisa demanding in the months after he'd returned home.

"Not hiding," he'd say cheerfully over the phone as he'd headed for the door to go for a bike ride or swim in the ocean. Concentrating on the breathing, the muscle movement; a focus on each minute system that pumped life through his body became something he craved. As a way to escape from memories he did not want to relive? No. Self-healing, that was all. Strengthening of the mind and body was not hiding. Was it?

He shut the thoughts down and guided the convertible to the hospital, sliding into a parking space. Angela hopped out before he could get the door for her. Just as well. His pride still stung.

They made their way up to the third floor and found Patricia Lane gone. The nurse directed them to the dialysis clinic. When they arrived, they ducked their heads inside. Patricia sat with a gaunt young man, holding his hand. It was obviously a private moment, so they were turning to go when she spotted Dan.

She looked at them in surprise. "What are you doing here?"

"Just had a question for you. We'll wait outside. Don't hurry."

The young man opened his eyes, examining Dan and Angela curiously. "Nice to see some different faces," he said. "This place has all the charm of a mausoleum."

"This is my son-in-law, Lance," she said.

Dan remembered hearing from Jeb that Lance was ill, but Dan had not known her well enough to ask about the particulars. She'd come on board at the hospital only a few months before he'd deployed, so there wasn't a close bond between them.

Angela looked at Lance intently, as if she recognized him, but she did not comment beyond the pleasantries. They made polite introductions and excused themselves to wait in the hallway.

Patricia joined them after a few moments.

"I'm sorry to intrude," Dan said. "How is your son-in-law?"

"Failing, if you want the honest truth," she said. He saw lines of fatigue and worry etched into her face. "Only one of his kidneys is functioning. Barely."

"Is he a transplant candidate?"

She sighed. "He would be if he could stop drinking. He's failed two blood tests so far, so he's disqualified himself from getting a transplant until he can prove he's sticking with his treatment plan. Dialysis is our only option right now." She sighed. "As a surgeon, I would make the same decision. Why give a precious organ to someone who continues to abuse their body?"

He was not sure how to respond.

She shrugged. "Sorry to sound bitter. Lance was married to my daughter, and she was killed in a wreck shortly after their baby was born. So Lance is the only parent Sadie has left. It kills me that I can't fix him and he can't fix his own addiction no matter how many treatment programs he's attempted. Maybe it wouldn't be so frustrating if I wasn't in this line of work. Doctor, heal thy own." She shook her head.

Dan put a hand on her shoulder. "I'm sorry."

"Don't be. He's a fighter, and so am I. We will get through this for Sadie's sake. But you didn't come here to talk to me about Lance. What can I do for you?"

"I wanted to ask you about Ralph Pickford. Is he a patient of yours?"

She blinked, looking away. "No."

"Then why was he in your exam room the day Lila Brown ran away from here?"

"Ralph was confused. He's been a local fixture in town for the past year. He comes in often to warm up or use the bathroom. That day he began to wander the halls, insisting he needed lunch." She smiled. "We got him some gelatin and a soup cup."

"That was kind of you," Angela said.

She shrugged. "I don't like to see anyone go hungry. Why are you asking about him?"

"Hope I'm not interrupting." Lieutenant Torrey, wearing chinos and a black jacket, walked up. He handed Patricia a cup of coffee, holding another cup for himself.

"Oh, that's why Lance looks familiar," Angela said to Torrey. "He has your chin and eyes. He's your son, isn't he?"

Dan was thunderstruck that he had not seen the resemblance before. He'd known Lance was Patricia's son-in-law, but he'd never suspected that Torrey was Lance's father.

"Good detective work," Torrey said. "Yes, he's my son. Patricia and I share a granddaughter. Sadie's the best thing that ever happened to me." He took out his cell phone. "I know I'm partial, but isn't that the cutest face you ever did see?"

A little girl, probably three years old, grinned on the screen, curly hair, brown eyes, freckles.

"She is pretty cute, all right," Angela said.

His smile softened the heavy creases in his face as he nodded to Patricia. "Came to check on my boy. How's he doing?"

Patricia's face was grim. "Hanging in there. Amyloidosis is getting him down."

Torrey looked at them. "Stiffness and discomfort from too much protein in the blood. Gets deposited on joints or tendons." He shrugged. "I'm getting to be an expert since this all happened to his mother, too, before it killed her. Genes are nothing to laugh at. So why are you here asking Patricia questions about Ralph Pickford?"

"We think he's got something to do with Tank and the Grubers."

Torrey's eyes narrowed. "So why ask Patricia?"

"I saw Ralph here at the hospital the day Lila bolted," Dan said.

Patricia shoved her hands in the pockets of her white coat. "But that was just coincidental. He's not my patient, so I can't really tell them anything."

"I know he was treated at the clinic," Dan said. "I'll ask Lila about it."

"Here's a thought, Doc. How about I ask her?" Torrey snapped. "Or is that getting in the way of your amateur hour?"

"Max…" Patricia said, a warning in her tone.

"No, really. I mean you seem like you two got

this whole thing handled." His eyes blazed. "You're everywhere. At the hospital, the beach, Lila's house. I'm not even sure why we need cops in this town with you detectives on the case."

Dan straightened. "We're all looking for the truth. That puts us both on the same side."

"Does it now?" Torrey said. "'Cause it sure feels a lot like you two are doing whatever suits your fancy."

"That's because of me," Angela said. "I'm trying to help Tank, and Dr. Blackwater got caught up in it."

"Tank will be thrilled to know he's got so many people on his side, if he ever has the backbone to show up, that is. I guess I'll just go find some paperwork to fill out. Maybe I can issue some parking tickets. Let me know how it all turns out when you solve the case, huh?" Torrey whirled on his heel and stalked off.

"I apologize for him." Patricia sighed. "He's under a lot of pressure about Lance. I mean, he's already gone through it once, like he said, and watched his wife die. Alcoholism runs in his family on the paternal side. He's been sober for twenty years, but it kills him to see Lance turn into an alcoholic, too. He and Lance have never gotten along, but Lance and Sadie are all the family he's got. Max would do anything for Sadie."

"Tough situation."

"Yes." She gazed in the direction he'd gone.

"People will do whatever it takes for their children, you know? I would for my Elizabeth, if she were still alive."

Dan saw the wealth of sadness in Patricia's eyes. What had it cost her to lose her daughter? Her only child.

Angela must have seen the same thing. "We're very sorry that Lance is ill. I apologize if we've made the situation more difficult for you or the lieutenant."

She shrugged. "We'll make it through. I've got to get back to work now."

Dan led Angela back to the elevator, his thoughts churning.

She watched him. "What are you thinking?"

"Ralph just happened to be on the third floor asking Patricia Lane for a lunch handout? He didn't go to the cafeteria or help himself to the free coffee in the lobby?"

"Unlikely story, I agree."

"But why would she lie?"

As they stepped off the elevator, Angela's phone rang. They went outside, away from the building, and she put it on speakerphone.

"Betty Hernandez reportedly lives in an apartment in Tijuana," Marco said. "We've got an address and phone for her, so we're following up on that, but so far there's no answer. Oliver Clark is dead, car wreck, three months ago, in Mexico."

She told him about Ralph Pickford and their conversation with Patricia Lane and Lieutenant Torrey.

"Going to catch a flight to Tijuana right now. Be back by tonight. Can you two stay out of trouble until we get back?"

"Yes," she said.

"Why is that hard for me to believe?"

"We're going to work on finding Ralph Pickford's whereabouts," Dan put in.

"Even though Torrey is pitching a fit?"

Dan shrugged. "We will stay out of his way."

"And we will talk to Mrs. Guzman, too," Angela said quietly.

"We may just be chasing our tails here," Marco said. "We've got nothing solid. You really think these names Guzman gave us mean anything?"

"I don't know," he said as Angela clicked off.

But he felt an urgent need to find out.

Lila Brown did not answer her cell phone. Again. Angela put down the phone in frustration. "And she's not at the clinic, either, or at least she's not answering. What do we do now?"

Dan drummed his fingers on the steering wheel. "I believe it's time to get some hot dogs."

Angela checked her watch. "It's only eleven. It's not lunchtime."

"It's always the right time for some information."

"Oh, I see. I should have thought of that."

He drove back to the beach, and once again they approached Bill, the hot dog vendor.

"I'm looking for someone," Dan said. "Guy named Ralph Pickford. Know him?"

"Sure, Doc Man. He's a regular. Lives on the beach when it's warm."

"And when it's not?"

Bill served up two hot dogs. "Whatcha going to do to him?"

"Just ask him some questions and maybe buy him a hot dog."

Bill seemed satisfied. "Abandoned pumping station. It's dry in some places. No one bothers him down there."

"Can you tell me where to find it?" Dan said.

"All boarded up, but you can get to it same way Bill does."

"How's that?"

"Right up the beach. Find the cement runoff pipe." He looked over the top of his half glasses. "Ralph's a popular guy these days."

"How's that?"

"You weren't the only folks looking for him today."

"Who else?"

"Young lady. Headed up there about a half hour ago."

Angela sucked in a breath. "Dark hair? Brown eyes?"

He nodded. "Ralph sure does have the charm, doesn't he? All this attention."

Angela shot a look at Dan as they walked away. Ralph had something. She hoped it was answers.

"Has to be Lila," Dan said, staring up the beach. "I'm going to go see."

"I'm right behind you."

He stopped. "At the risk of being told off again, Marco doesn't want you prancing around in abandoned pumping stations, and he's right."

"I've been in far worse places." His gray eyes met hers. So had he. With bullets and death and suffering.

He opened his mouth, but she reached up and pressed a finger to his lips. "I'll leave a message on Marco's phone and tell him what we're up to. I can do the same for Torrey, if you feel like that's a good idea."

Uncertainty flickered in his eyes, and he took hold of her fingers, guiding them over his cheek. The feel of his warm skin on her palm sent tingles through her body. Finally he pressed a kiss to her palm.

"I don't know who to trust, and that's what worries me. This reminds me of Kandahar. Hard to tell the enemies from the friendlies."

She lingered in his grasp for a moment more. What comfort to be connected to a man she realized was much more than a friend. Her own thoughts surprised her. *More than a friend?*

No. She pulled away. She was here not for emotional entanglements, which would cripple her further, but to do whatever she could to help Julio's brother.

"I've got an idea," he said. "I'll send a message to Jeb about what we're doing. He can be our local safety net and call for help in a couple of hours if he doesn't hear from us. We'll leave Torrey out of it for the moment. And I'll grab a flashlight from the car."

"Okay."

She was grateful when he turned away to message Jeb, taking the time to try to calm her thoughts. Her palm still tingled from the kiss he'd placed there. Find Tank and go home. But what waited for her back in Coronado? Still the same crippling memories, a job she could not do, a God she could no longer reach.

"Ready?" she said brightly when he disconnected.

"Let's go make like detectives," he said. "You can be Watson."

"Uh-uh," she said. "You're the doctor, after all."

"Right you are, Sherlock," he said.

Sand infiltrated her shoes as they hiked a mile up the beach, past bodyboarders who did not seem to mind the chilly January temperatures. The morning was giving way to afternoon. Except for the occasional beachcomber, they were alone as they arrived at a crescent-shaped section of cliff.

"There," Dan said, pointing.

She'd almost missed it. A thick cement pipe

jutted from the rock, some six feet wide, nearly hidden by a screen of bushes. The water did not reach the pipe, but the bottom was damp, probably from last night's storm.

"You think Ralph is in there?" She suppressed a shudder as Dan shone his flashlight into the mouth of the pipe.

"It would make a good shelter from the elements and probably not too much trouble with people dropping by." He ducked his head and ventured in a little farther. "Be right back." The shadows swallowed him up, as if he were being devoured by an enormous snake.

She steeled her shoulders, steadied her trembling knees. "Come on, Angela. You used to go caving with Dad all the time. Get yourself together and move out." After a deep breath, she ducked into the darkness right behind him.

SEVENTEEN

The pipe sloped gradually upward. Dan had to duck his head and shoulders to continue his progress, his hair grazing against the cement. When the grade steepened, he got on his hands and knees and crawled. Angela was glad she was not quite as tall. She did not need to assume a crawling position until several feet into their adventure. Then her palms and knees ached from the impact of the hard surface.

"There's a platform up ahead," he said, voice hushed.

"Good. My knees are killing me."

After a few more feet, Dan climbed up onto a cement floor and offered a hand to her. They found themselves in a narrow corridor filled with rusted pipes and tanks. The ceiling was low, some eight feet, enough room for Dan to stand. Blackened metalwork splayed backward into the darkness. Dan shone the flashlight; the beam was too weak to fully pierce the darkness.

"It leads back into another room, I think."

Angela stayed close, peering around. "I don't see any sign of Ralph. No indication that he really does hang out down here."

"No sign of Lila, either. Could be I got some bogus information along with my hot dogs."

It occurred to her that Bill's loyalties might belong elsewhere. Was he getting a payoff from Gruber or his brother? Maybe from Torrey even? *Hard to tell the friendlies from the enemies.* Her stomach muscles clamped into a hard ball. The air was stuffy, muggy with humidity and scented with the tang of rusting metal. Sweat prickled her brow, and she tried to shake the feeling that she and Dan were entombed in a cement labyrinth, moving in deeper with every step. Cold shocked her feet as she stepped into a puddle. Was it water driven in by the storm, or was there a leak somewhere, the ocean gradually seeping in to drown them? She forced herself forward. *Come on Angela. One foot in front of the other.*

Dan stopped so abruptly, she plowed into his back, cheek impacting his hard shoulder.

"What?" she whispered.

"Look at that." He beamed the light across the ceiling pipes, and she heard his breath catch.

"Oh, man," he groaned.

She looked closer. A gleam of red eyes peered back at her. She let out a sigh of relief. "Whew. Just a rat."

"Just a rat?" he said, incredulous. "Do you know what kind of diseases these things carry? How about the bubonic plague?"

The disgust in his voice amused her. "I think they've got antibiotics for that now."

"Salmonella, rat-bite fever." He ticked off the diseases on his fingers. "Leptospirosis, tapeworms, typhus."

She tried to keep her face serious. "So I guess this isn't a good time to tell you I had a pet rat as a kid?"

His aghast expression nearly made her burst out laughing.

"Why would anyone want to keep a vermin as a pet?"

Angela shrugged. "Her name was Sparkles, and she used to climb up a rope in her cage and ring a bell when she wanted to go out."

He closed his eyes as if pained. "You're killing me."

"Sorry, I didn't know you had a fear of rats."

"It's not a fear. It's a logical aversion to organisms that carry pestilence."

"I stand corrected." She giggled, enjoying his discomfiture more than she probably should have.

Ducking very low to creep under the pipes, Dan moved ahead muttering about rodent-borne diseases.

There was still no sign of any human activity in the place except theirs. After a few more steps, Dan stopped.

"I think we're spinning our wheels. There's not one scrap of a clue to indicate anyone is here but us."

Angela did not need further encouragement. "Okay. Chalk it up to a dead end."

Dan sighed. "I thought we were finally going to get some answers."

They'd turned to go when a woman's cry echoed through the space.

Dan whirled the flashlight. "Where'd it come from?"

"The back," Angela whispered. "That way."

Dan rushed forward, skirting a massive rusted pipe and stepping over stacks of piled metal. She scrambled after him, trying to keep her head low to avoid the various metal and cement formations that jutted down from the ceiling. Her heart pounded a strong tempo against her ribs, the sound of that scream ringing in her ears.

It had to be Lila. And someone else? Her memory dredged up the feel of her attacker, the knife cutting into her back. Swallowing hard, she kept going. They raced as quickly as they could to the far end of the pumping station until they encountered an unyielding wall of damp cement. Nothing but shadows and the stench of rust, stronger now. No sign of Lila or Ralph.

Their breathing rasped loudly in the darkness, the only sound except for the drip of water and the skittering of a rat overhead.

"Where is she?" Angela breathed.

Dan trailed his fingers along the cement. "There must be another door, a tunnel, something."

Then she spotted it. "Down there."

Dan lowered the flashlight beam to reveal a hole some four feet across, cut into the cement wall at floor level. At one time there must have been a small door to seal it off, but now it was gone, leaving its contents unguarded. The perfect hiding place.

A play of light flicked through the darkness on the other side, the beam of a flashlight. Another cry, this time softer, a sob.

Dan pocketed his own flashlight and crawled in. "Lila," he yelled. "It's Dan. I'm coming in."

Angela gritted her teeth and followed, the chill of the cement floor seeping into her body. The room they'd wriggled into was small, six feet by six feet, and dark, except for the soft glow of a battery-powered lantern and the weak beam of a flashlight. Lila held the flashlight with both hands, as if she meant to protect herself from them, her face eerie, scared.

"How did you get here?" she asked, eyes wide.

"Climbed in, same as you," Dan said. "What's wrong?"

She bit her lip and slowly lowered the beam of the flashlight. It revealed a figure on the floor, face-down, an old man with gray hair. He was very still. Angela's heart sank.

"It's Ralph," Lila whispered. "Ralph Pickford."

Dan dove to his knees, fingers searching Ralph's neck for a pulse.

"He's alive," Dan said. "Pulse is faint."

Angela immediately dropped down beside him and took hold of the flashlight so Dan could do an examination. He lifted the edge of Ralph's coat and peered at his back. "There's a bandaged area here, but no bleed through. I need to turn him over. Lila, hold the flashlight so Angela can help."

As gently as they could, the rolled him over onto his back. Ralph's eyes were closed, his face peaceful as though he could be taking a nap. She guessed he might be in his midsixties, but his weathered skin and the creases burrowed into his forehead indicated his life had been lived largely outside. His clothes were neat, as if they had been purchased recently. On the floor nearby was a box filled with canned food, a loaf of bread and a gallon container of water. Dan examined his torso.

Lila's breath was shallow and panicky. "Tank called me. He's taking Cora to Mexico. He told me he'd given you Ralph's name. I wanted to tell Ralph to run, to get out of town before it was too late. He is a nice man. Nice..." Her voice trailed off.

"Too late for what?" Angela said.

Lila bit her lip. "Ralph should have left town after. Why did he have to stay in Cobalt Cove?"

"Lila, what are you talking about?" Angela said sternly.

"I hate this town," she whispered. "I never should have come here. Now I'm trapped."

"More light," Dan snapped. Angela took the

flashlight from Lila's unresisting hand and shone both on Ralph.

"Does he have a head injury?" Angela said. "Did he trip over one of these pipes?"

Dan stopped at the neck. "Angela, hold the light here."

She crouched, sucking in a breath as she saw what he was staring at. Ralph's neck was bruised and swollen, the fingermarks showing livid against the pale skin of his throat.

"It wasn't a head injury," he said slowly, eyes riveted to hers in the darkness. "He's been throttled."

Dan knew Ralph wouldn't last long on the cold cement floor. His pulse was already faint, body shocked from the choking he'd received and possibly other injuries Dan couldn't detect.

Lila stood with her hands to her mouth. Angela held the flashlight. Her gaze went suddenly to the floor. "The water."

It took a moment for him to realize the truth. The water was rising. The occasional puddles were now expanding, joining together as they spilled over the floor. "Someone must have opened a pipe somewhere."

Lila gulped. "We're going to drown in here."

"No. The level's rising slowly. We have time to get out," Angela said.

"Are you sure?" Lila whispered.

Angela nodded. "But what about Ralph?"

Dan got to his feet. "I'll carry him."

Angela stood. "Lila, you're going to climb out of here first," she commanded. "I need to help Dan with Ralph."

Lila didn't answer, so Angela thrust both flashlights into her hands and pointed her to the small opening.

Still she didn't move, staring at the water pouring over the tops of her shoes.

Angela took her by the shoulders. "We need to help Ralph. One foot in front of the other, okay?"

Slowly Lila seemed to find her senses. She nodded.

Angela came back to Dan. "What's the best way to do this, Doctor?"

Doctor. The darkness and the sheer lunacy of the situation took him back to Kandahar. For a moment, he could not speak. Ralph's life, the divine gift, was in his hands, and he found he did not want it there. Somebody else should save him. Somebody who did not already have a notebook filled with the names of those he had not been able to rescue, the names he'd memorized, poring over them until they'd lodged inside his soul.

Mark Javier.

Dino Smith.

Lenny Kesselman.

The names scrolled through his mind.

Julio Guzman.

He was not a doctor anymore; he did not want to be. Then Angela reached out and laid her hand on his shoulder. Slowly he brought her into focus. She caught his eyes with hers, a look that seemed to reach into the core of him. Slowly she held her other hand out and cupped his cheek. "Just tell me what to do," she said.

He did not want to resume the role of doctor, but there was a patient who would die if he didn't. Angela's touch grounded him.

Just get him out. Get them out. God's got this, even if you don't.

He took a breath. "I'll carry him under the shoulders and try to keep his neck as steady as I can. You take his feet and tell me if I'm about to run into anything. We'll stop in a few minutes and I'll check his breathing. The hard part's going to be getting him through this hole."

Lila went ahead and shone the light so they could see. Somehow, slithering, grasping and pushing, they got Ralph through the narrow opening. Dan hoisted his shoulders, and Angela struggled with his booted feet. The water was pooling now above their ankles.

A thundering sound filled the space. The source soon became clear. One of the massive vertical pipes was vomiting water at an alarming rate.

"How did that happen?" she yelled over the noise. "Did the pipe fail?"

Dan shook his head. "I think it had help from someone."

Lila was trembling now as they splashed on. She cried out, falling to one knee, one of the flashlights whirling out of her hand. The flow yanked it away. "Sorry," she said as she got to her feet again.

With only the single flashlight beam, the going was treacherous.

"Stop," he heard Angela yell a moment before he was about to run into a low pipe. He adjusted, crouching over Ralph's body, and made it by. They were almost at the outer platform when the other flashlight began to fade.

"Only a little farther," Dan called. "Keep going."

Dan thought he heard something. He strained to make it out over the sound of the rush and the rasping of his own breath. After signaling, he sank down on his knees, holding Ralph above the water level and taking his pulse. His own fingertips were so cold he had to chafe the feeling back into them. He pressed them there, seeking that reassuring flutter of the divine. *Hang on, Ralph.*

He was rising, heaving his end of the load, when a look of horror dawned on Angela's face as she stared past him. He craned his neck to see what she was looking at. It was just a head at first, oddly illuminated by a swinging lantern. Then a set of narrow shoulders came into view as someone climbed up onto the platform.

EIGHTEEN

Lila gasped.

Peter Gruber stepped onto the platform and looked from her to Dan and Angela with their patient in tow. He didn't say a word but went to Lila and crushed her in an embrace, expression stricken.

"Are you okay?" he said. He held her at arm's length after a moment, put his lantern down and framed her face with his hands. "My poor girl. You shouldn't have come here. Are you sure you're not hurt?"

She shook her head.

He gave her a relieved smile. "Then I arrived just in time. I've got to get you out before you drown."

Lila looked utterly bewildered. "What… How did you know I was here?"

"No time now," Peter said, guiding her by the shoulders. He looked at Dan and Angela. "I'll get her out, call for an ambulance and then come back to help you. Take my lantern," he said, putting it on a flat chunk of cement.

Dan did not trust Peter Gruber one bit. He could tell from Angela's expression that she shared his feelings. They pulled Ralph up onto the platform as Peter led Lila away. Once they made it up onto the cement landing, they laid Ralph down. On hands and knees, they gasped for breath.

"You go on ahead," Dan said. "I'll carry him the rest of the way."

She shook her head. "Nope. I'm here until we get him out."

Her hair was dripping, shoulders quaking with the cold. The only spots of color on her face were those two green eyes, blazing with determination. He wished he had time to just stare at her, to drink in that incredible courage wrapped in a breathtakingly beautiful package. Instead he checked Ralph's pulse. He felt nothing, only the beginnings of panic in his own gut. After chafing and blowing on his fingertips, he tried again. No throb of heartbeat. Perhaps it was too faint for him to feel.

Kneeling, he put his cheek next to Ralph's.

"His heart's stopped, and he's not breathing." Dan immediately started compressions. "You have to go and make sure Peter called for an ambulance."

"No."

"Angela, please," he said, never ceasing the CPR. "We're safe from the water for a while, but time is running out."

"I...I don't want to leave you."

His gut, his heart, his body and mind all answered together. *And I don't want you to leave me, either.* But he was faced again with the dilemma that had haunted him since Kandahar. *Why did God give me the power to save, and the pain of watching when I can't?* Was he going to witness Ralph die in spite of his efforts?

"You have to go, Angela," he said, continuing compressions.

She placed her hand on his shoulder and closed her eyes, a frown puckering her brow. He knew she was praying for him and Ralph, and that tender gesture from a woman who felt so far-flung from God rendered him breathless. He felt hopeful, filled with the very presence of the God who would not quit, the God who pursued His children even into the darkest corners, the hopeless chasms. He felt new energy course through him.

When she finished, he saw that it had not been easy for her.

"Thank you, Chaplain," he whispered.

With an uncertain smile and one more squeeze of her hand, she ran into the darkness, sprinting across the platform and disappearing from view.

He was left alone. The rush of the water played a soothing counterpart to his compressions.

"Hey, Ralph," he said. "I'm sorry you were alone down here. Stay with me awhile, okay? We're going to do some praying, all right?"

And Dan did pray. He started with those he had not saved, their families.

Javier.

Smith.

Kesselman.

Guzman.

And he moved on to the others, as many as he could bring up. His hands continued to press against Ralph's chest, as he prayed for those engaged in their own kind of battle, the ones who came home alive but still fought every day for their wholeness. Jeb, Angela, so many souls tortured by what they'd endured, yearning for a peace they could not find.

"And for you, Ralph," he murmured. "Now we're going to pray for you."

He was still praying when Angela crawled back in, two paramedics right behind her. He gave them a quick overview and stepped away, exhausted, as they took over.

His arms ached from the compressions, his muscles depleted. Angela took his hand.

"Come on. Let's go."

"Wait," he said, turning to her. The noise from the paramedics faded away and once again they were cocooned in shadows, with nothing but the sound of the water. "You prayed for me, didn't you?"

She nodded.

"Tell me what you asked God for. Can you?"

She bit her lip. "I...I asked the Lord to give you the strength to do what He made you to do."

Flickers of emotion cascaded through his body like droplets of water.

What He made you to do. Joy hitched up his breath for a second as he reconnected to the vine, the power of the Father. "And when you prayed," he said carefully, "He gave you the strength to do what He made you to do."

Her mouth twitched, eyes filling. "I'm not sure."

He held her hands. "I'm sure."

"Why would He call me to minister and then watch me fall apart?"

"I don't know. Same reason He made me a doctor who can't save all his patients."

She stamped her foot. "Why would He do that?"

He smiled. "Beats me, but I'm going to ask Him someday."

She laughed, an airy, bubbling peal of laughter that seemed to break through the gloom and ignite a sunrise in his heart. He pulled her to him, rocking her back and forth, until he felt her face upturned to his.

He kissed her forehead, her cheek. Her mouth hovered soft and inviting, a fraction of an inch away. Though he wanted to press a kiss there, he knew she was not ready.

And you're not, either, he told himself. Not ready for love, ill prepared to offer up himself when he was not completely sure who he was anymore. Her head dropped, and she let out a quiet sigh. He took her hand, his own heart still beating hard in his chest.

"Ready?"

She nodded.

They climbed out, blinking against the sun. It seemed like a very long time since they'd crawled into that tunnel. Medics wrapped blankets around them and checked vitals. He watched them load Ralph into a waiting ambulance and speed away. It was unlikely the hospital would be able to revive the man. Dan swallowed. Though he'd never spoken a word to Ralph Pickford, he found himself desperately hoping he would live.

"Over to You now, God," he whispered as he shook off the blanket.

Angela's heart throbbed and, even with the blanket, she was cold to the bone. What had happened in that underground tomb? They'd found Lila and a stricken Ralph; someone had tried to drown them perhaps. But strangest of all, in that horrible place, she'd found the courage to pray again. It did not crowd away the numbing of her soul, but it had changed something. She'd felt a thread of divine connection, the barest glimmer. Did it mean healing at long last? Or false hope? She wished she had the courage to talk to Dan about it.

Her thoughts were interrupted by Peter Gruber, who strode over while the medics checked Lila for injury.

"You two okay?"

"What were you doing down there?" Angela demanded, relieved to put aside her confusing thoughts.

Peter looked offended. "Saving you and Lila."

Dan joined her. "We would have made it out just fine by ourselves."

Peter shrugged. "Whatever you say."

"How did you know Lila was down there?"

"I heard her talking to Tank on the phone. He just can't leave her alone. I knew he would go after her, so I've been following her to protect her."

"From Tank? Or your brother?"

"My brother has never done anything but help Lila, and she'll tell you the same thing. I met Lila when I guest lectured at her dental hygiene school. I told Harry about her, and he helped her get through, hired her to work as my hygienist."

"Don't you hire your own people?" Dan asked.

He colored. "Ah, yes, usually, but financially things have been difficult, so my brother employs her technically, though she works for me."

"Your brother is a real philanthropist. How does he pay for everything?"

Peter stiffened. "Not that it's your business, but he inherited a trucking company from my uncle. He's worked real hard to make it a success. He's going to retire soon. Go live with his daughter and grandkids, who adore him, by the way."

"So Harry is a stand-up guy, huh?" Dan said.

"Yes, he is, in spite of what he's endured. He watched his wife die waiting for a kidney transplant that never came because the doctors gave them away to other people, richer people."

Dan shook his head. "That's not how it works. The OPTN manages the transplant list." He looked at Angela. "That's the Organ Procurement and Transplantation Network, and it's based on need, not income or anything else."

Peter huffed. "Don't try to have that conversation with Harry. He'll cut you into a million pieces. It's up to the OPTN who gets a transplant, but it's up to the transplant centers to collect payment. And if you can't pay, too bad."

Dan frowned. "Not true. Transplant centers have financial assistance to help patients arrange payment."

"Maybe, but even if they had put Harry's wife first on the list and she got the organ, he would have been ruined trying to pay for the surgery. Or the antirejection drugs that follow. Those are sometimes more costly than the surgery."

"It sounds like Harry worked with the wrong transplant center."

"You doctors," Peter said. "So quick to put yourself on a pedestal and cast the blame elsewhere."

"All right, let's leave the topic for now," Angela said. "Someone choked Ralph almost to death. Who do you think that was, Peter?"

He shrugged. "I don't even know the guy."

"And how about the valve?" She pushed the wet hair from her face. "The fire department people said someone opened it up from above while we were down there. Who would want to drown us?"

"I told you. Tank is obsessed with Lila. He wants to own her. She's told him to leave her alone, and he can't accept it. He would rather see her die than be with anyone else."

Anyone else? Angela thought. Did Peter think of himself as the man Lila really belonged with? Was Tank the delusional one, or Peter?

"I've discussed it with Lieutenant Torrey. He believes me that Tank is a stalker."

That might explain the meeting between the two men that Jeb had witnessed. Peter hastened back to Lila, ushering her away from the medics and over to his car, which was parked near the hot dog vendor. They passed the police, who were just arriving. Angela braced herself for another round of questioning. Torrey was not going to be pleased at their latest escapade.

"Peter acts like Lila's husband," she said, watching Peter bend close to arrange the blanket around Lila's shoulders, talking quietly in her ear.

"Does she feel that way, too?" Dan said.

Angela shook her head. "He may be in love with Lila, but I saw the look on her face. She doesn't return the feeling."

"Why go along with it then?" Dan said. "Why work for the guy and string him along?"

Their eyes locked.

"There's only one emotion that I can think of that's as strong as love," Dan said.

Angela nodded slowly. "Fear."

Angela was so exhausted when she returned to her hotel room, she could only manage to pull on some dry clothes and throw herself on the bed. She did not wake up until her cell buzzed sometime later.

"I can't take it anymore. I'm ready to help you bring him down."

Angela fought off the fuzziness. "Lila? Is that you?"

"Can you come meet me? Please? I'll be at the clinic in forty-five minutes to get my things. Then I'm out of here."

"Yes, but can't we talk on the phone?"

"No. I'm going to give you the information, and then I'm leaving and I'm never coming back. Quinn and I are going to find someplace to live where the Grubers can't find us."

"But—"

"I'll be at the clinic in forty-five minutes," she repeated. "If you haven't come by then…"

Lila disconnected.

Marco and Donna were still en route home from the airport, but she texted anyway so they would get the message when they landed. Her nerves were buzzing, hyperalert. She wanted to go put an end to it, to find the piece that would help Tank, and she wanted to do it alone. Her growing feelings for Dan confused her; added to the pile of emotions that had built up inside. Her heart was just too frayed, too tattered to handle her confusion over Dan.

But Angela was not a careless person, nor overly impulsive, at least she had not been before Kandahar. It was prudence, good judgment that made her place a call to Dan, her pulse pounding while she waited for him to pick up. He did not answer, so she left a message and checked her watch.

Forty minutes left. She began to pace, checking her phone to see if she had missed a message from Dan. Nothing.

The time ticked down. Thirty minutes. It would take her ten to drive over. She stalled for another few minutes.

At twenty minutes to the meeting time, she grabbed her keys.

She would go, park on the curb in a nice public spot and wait for Dan. They'd approach Lila together, and if Lila left before Dan arrived, Angela would follow her.

She rushed out, surprised to see through the window that it was raining again. Ten minutes left. There was no time to go back for a jacket.

She hit the elevator button and hopped inside. Just before the doors closed, someone jogged up. Her breath caught as Harry Gruber stepped in.

"Hello, Chaplain," he said, pressing the button to close the doors.

NINETEEN

Dan changed quickly into dry clothes and drove immediately back to the hospital, where they told him that Ralph was still alive, barely. The emergency room doctors had managed to start his heart again.

A fact kept poking at Dan's mind. The bandage on Ralph's back, a newly changed bandage. Why did the detail keep resurfacing? He knew they would have done a quick scan to check for internal bleeding. If Dan was charming enough, maybe one of technicians would share some info.

He saw Patricia Lane start down the hallway. She tried to reverse directions when she caught sight of him, but he confronted her anyway.

"You heard about Ralph?"

She nodded.

"He's still alive," Dan said.

"I know." She looked exhausted, eyes red rimmed as if she might have been crying. "It's terrible what happened to him. He is a kind man, gentle. He doesn't deserve this."

"He had a bandaged wound on his lower back."

She seemed to go rigid, as if a cold wind had blown through the corridor.

"Was he seen here? Treated at this hospital for kidney problems of any kind?"

She shook her head. "Not that I'm aware of. Not by me, anyway."

"But you would know. If he'd been a kidney patient, you would know."

"Yes. I would."

He searched her face. "Patricia, what is going on here?"

"Just ordinary hospital business." Her mouth twitched.

"Then why do you look scared?"

He saw her throat convulse. "Maybe because my son-in-law is gravely ill? Isn't that enough reason to be scared?"

"It's just odd that Ralph was here at this hospital talking to you, a kidney specialist, yet you say you never treated him."

"I didn't. There is no record in the system of him having been my patient. The police can confirm that."

"Lieutenant Torrey? Would he contradict you? The woman who is trying to save his son?"

Her eyes flamed. "I resent the implication, Dr.

Blackwater. You are impugning my reputation and now Max's, too. Who do you think you are?"

"Just a guy trying to get to the core of a bad situation."

"You're imagining some sort of plot where there isn't any."

"Am I?"

"You have no rights, no authority here." She stepped back. "You don't belong in this hospital, Dr. Blackwater, until your leave is over, if it is ever going to be over. I'm going to have to ask you to go."

"Who are you covering up for?"

"Do I need to call security to provide you an escort?"

He stared at her. "I know you're a good doctor, Patricia, and I know you wouldn't be involved in anything unless you didn't have a choice. Let me help you."

She reached for her phone. "I'm calling security."

"No need," he said. "I'll go." He walked away, feeling Patricia's gaze following his progress. He'd always felt comfort from the tidy hallways, the open doors where people were receiving the life-saving help they needed. Now? The air closed in on him, oppressive, ominous.

Outside, he saw the message on his phone from Angela and jogged to his truck. In fifteen minutes he was at the clinic. Angela had not yet arrived.

He sat, mulling over the encounter with Patricia.

"You're imagining some sort of plot where there isn't any."

Was he? There could be many different explanations for the bandage on Ralph's back. Had he just alienated a colleague with his wild innuendo? A brilliant, hardworking colleague who was suffering under her own heavy burden?

Jeb called him a moment later. "You were right. I've got a friend in the imaging department. She did the scan on Ralph Pickford. She tells me, off the record of course, that Ralph had a kidney removed in the recent past, probably a couple of months or so ago. How did you know that?"

A cold ball crystallized inside him.

"Thanks, Jeb," he said, hanging up without answering.

A kidney removed. And he'd been at the hospital talking to Patricia Lane, a kidney surgeon who claimed she was merely giving him lunch, nothing more.

"Oh, Patricia," he muttered. "What have you gotten yourself into?"

Angela felt the press of the cold metal wall behind her. Harry Gruber stood in front of the doors and pushed the emergency stop button. Her body went rigid with fear. "Let me out," she demanded.

"Not until we've had our chat," he said.

She frantically pressed buttons on her phone, only to see the no-signal message come up. *Stay calm*, she told herself. *You know some basic self-defense. You can handle this.*

He wore a tan jacket, his hands balled into the pockets. Holding a weapon?

She edged as far away as she could.

He stared at her, not speaking, until a bead of sweat ran down the side of her face.

"You've been so busy gallivanting around Cobalt Cove," he finally said, "we have hardly had a moment to talk. How do you like our little town, by the way? It's not for me, living on the Central Coast, but my wife loved it. I'm more of a full-time sun guy, which is why I'm going to retire in San Diego with my daughter, Jen." He smiled. "Jen's an amazing woman. Single parent raising kids and a CPA to boot. She turned out well in spite of me."

She gulped, forcing strength into her voice that she did not feel. "I don't like being intimidated in elevators."

"Am I intimidating you?" He frowned. "I thought we were just talking."

"I know you're trying to kill Tank, and you've got Lila running scared, no matter what your brother says."

"Oh, my brother." Harry sighed. "How can a man smart enough to obtain a dental degree be so incredibly dense? He actually believes Lila has feelings for him. That she'll marry him someday and he'll be a loving daddy to her boy. Even if he hadn't gambled all his financial security away, she has nothing for him but pity, and he's the only one who can't see that."

"So why is Lila afraid to leave here?"

He shrugged. "I've no idea. Perhaps Peter is right and Tank Guzman really is stalking her."

"I think you know the real reason."

"And I think," he said, leaning forward, his breath sour, "that you should go home, back to Coronado, back to your sisters, your widowed mother and your niece and finish your leave at home in your little apartment."

She jerked in surprise.

He smiled. "So you think you're the only one who can pry into people's lives? You and your family and the doctor can ask questions about me and my clinic? My dead wife? My daughter?" His voice went hard and flat, brimming with suppressed rage. "I know about you, too. I know you are damaged goods, Chaplain. I know you're here trying to escape your guilt because Tank's brother died when it should have been you."

The accusation struck at her.

He shook his head, a pitying look on his face. "You know what? You can't escape that guilt. He's dead. You're not. No amount of scurrying around pretending to be a detective is going to change that. You know it's true. That's why you can't be a chaplain anymore, isn't it? How can you tell everyone about the forgiveness of God when you know deep down you can't forgive yourself?" He came close enough that she could see the broken capillaries on his cheeks. She readied a foot to kick out at him.

"I may be dealing with what happened in Afghanistan, but I can still tell a lie when I hear one, and you are a first-class liar," she muttered.

His mouth tightened as he watched her.

"I'm going to help Tank," she forced out through lips stiff with fear. "And we're going to bring you down."

He stopped, eyes wide for a minute, and then he laughed. "Bring me down? Me? Harry Gruber, the philanthropist who provides free medical care? The honest Joe who runs a trucking company and pays fair wages and benefits to his employees? The good brother who's bent over backward to support his brother and Lila Brown so she can raise her kid? That guy?"

"Yes," she said. "That guy."

He smiled. "All right. If you want to throw away your life, go ahead, but you're not going to damage mine."

The anger in his gaze told her she was making progress. Clenching her hands into fists to still the shaking, she said, "We're getting closer to the truth and it's got you rattled—doesn't it? That's why you're here on this elevator, trying to scare me. Tank got away, and we're closing in, ready to crack your perfect facade."

He raised his hand suddenly as if he would strike her.

She threw up an arm to block the blow, but it didn't come.

Harry stopped. "Oh, I'm sorry. I forgot you've been attacked recently. Does it hurt? The knife wound on your back?"

Her scalp prickled as her memory took her back to that moment, lying helpless beneath the knife. Harry's knife, there was no doubt in her mind. She thought she could see the edge of a bruise on his forehead under his hair where she'd bashed him with her head.

"You should be more careful," he said soothingly. "You might wind up like poor Ralph Pickford. I understand someone tried to strangle him."

You did, she thought. *But why?*

He frowned in thought. "And Lila, so close to getting blown up, burned to death."

"You can't terrorize me," she breathed.

"Oh, I don't have to." His gaze locked on her face. "You're already terrified. I can see it in your eyes."

Her lungs refused to work properly. It was agony to get a breath against the wild firing of her fear, the slamming of her heart against her ribs.

It should have been you...

Does it hurt? The knife wound on your back...

Terrified.

He pressed the elevator button, and it slowly headed down. "Go back to Coronado, Chaplain, while you still can."

* * *

She ran out to the parking lot, sucking in deep breaths of air, jerking her head around to see any sign of Harry Gruber. She flinched as a car zoomed up and came to an abrupt halt. Then Dan's arms were around her, and she lost all sense of control. She hardly felt him lift her into the passenger seat. He stood in the open door.

"You can get through this," he said. "Squeeze my hands."

She tried, but her body seemed to have no will of its own. It was as if her mind were imprisoned somewhere dark and terrifying.

"We'll do it together." He squeezed her fingers for a slow count of five and then relaxed.

After several moments of the gentle pressure to her hands, she was able to squeeze back. Her breaths became less shuddering, and she grew aware of her surroundings. The late afternoon sun poked through the clouds, outlining Dan's strong shoulders and revealed his look of concern tinged with quiet confidence.

You can get through this.

She continued to breathe and squeeze until she could get the words out, a stumbling gush of details that made his face go from concerned to enraged.

"I am going to see that guy in prison if it's the last thing I ever do on this planet," he said through gritted teeth.

"We've got to get to the clinic," she gasped. "Before Lila leaves. She may be the only person who can tell us what is truly going on with Gruber."

He raced to the driver's seat, gunned the engine and they took off. On the way she thought about Gruber and his connection to Lila. There were no threats made, Gruber had said, but Angela knew Lila was on the run for her life, as was Tank. Gruber was pulling strings she could not see, forcing them to comply through terror. The echo of that terror still rang through her own nerves.

Go back to Coronado, Chaplain, while you still can.

She wanted nothing more than to speed back to her lovely beach town, hide in her apartment and not come out for days, months even. But with Dan sitting beside her, shooting concerned looks at her every few moments, she knew she would not leave.

Partly for Lila.

Mostly for Tank.

But in some small way, she did not want to leave this man who somehow grounded her, reminded her that though she was unmoored from her career and her life, she was still invisibly tethered to God.

"Holy God," she whispered. "Help me. Help us."

TWENTY

Dan scanned the street. No sign of Lila, though he did not know if she would be on foot or in a borrowed car. The parking lot behind the clinic held a few vehicles, probably the last patients having their dental and eye exams on the top floor. There would be no activity in the clinic today.

He was driving around the lot for the second time when Angela's phone buzzed. She answered, hands shaking only a little, he was pleased to note.

Frowning, Angela put the call on speakerphone.

Marco's voice sounded fuzzy, filtered through a bad connection. "Found Betty Hernandez just before we left Tijuana. She's living with her sister. She didn't want to talk at first, but Donna buttered her up."

"My natural charm," Donna chimed in. "She's had a hard go of it since her husband left her. She was nearly homeless when she visited the clinic to have her tooth extracted. Now she is taking classes to learn to be a hairdresser and she's bought a sec-ondhand car."

"We were able to track Oliver Clark's last known address, too, but his family couldn't tell us much about any connection he might have had to the Grubers," Marco said.

"That's it?" Angela huffed. "That's all? What is the connection between Ralph, Oliver and Betty?"

"Two of them, probably all three, were seen by Dr. Peter Gruber at the clinic."

"Peter? But his brother's the criminal—I'm sure of it." Angela told them about finding Ralph and her confrontation in the elevator.

"I told you to stay put," Marco snapped.

"You can chew me out when you get back," Angela said. "Focus on the now. What else do these three have in common?"

"Ralph was wearing new clothes. You said Betty was taking classes. She bought a used car." Dan twirled the thoughts in his mind. "They all came into some money from somewhere."

"Look," Angela said, grabbing Dan's arm.

Lila jogged up the small flight of steps to the parking lot. She must have come from the basement level, and he wondered how she'd acquired keys to the off-limits area. Promising to call back imme-diately, Angela disconnected the call and waved to Lila.

Dan pulled over. Angela squeezed in the back and Lila took the passenger seat.

"Drive," she said, lips trembling. "Hurry. They can't see me here."

She ducked down, and he guided the convertible away several blocks before he pulled over and parked next to an empty, weed-filled lot.

"I'm leaving town as soon as I pick up my son," Lila said, fingers twisting the handle of her bag. "I went to the clinic to get some insurance."

"What insurance?"

"Pictures, but I couldn't get in. They've changed the locks."

"For where? What are you talking about?" Dan tried to keep the impatience from his voice without success. "What are you involved in, Lila?"

"I didn't do anything wrong," she said. "All I did was take blood samples. That's all."

"From your dental patients?" Angela asked.

She nodded. "Those that were clinic patients and needed a procedure done," she looked down. "The ones that were desperate for money. I told them we needed a blood sample to check for infection after we fixed their teeth, and most of them said yes. I did the blood draw, and then I gave the samples to Peter. That's all. I didn't do anything wrong. I didn't force anybody to do anything." Her eyes were wild.

Angela was staring at Lila. "And Peter did what with the samples?"

"Had them tested and typed. If Peter found a match and things worked out, the patients were offered money, a lot of money. It helped them. We were helping."

"They were given money if they were a match," Angela repeated. "A match for what?"

Lila sucked in a breath. "If their kidneys were a match for clients of Harry's, clients who needed a transplant."

Dan's breath caught. "Organ harvesting. That's what this is all about."

Lila nodded miserably.

Dan met Angela's eyes. "And the patients were paid handsomely for their kidneys, and probably told to leave town, I'm guessing."

She nodded.

"So Peter and Harry Gruber are running an illegal organ-harvesting business?" Angela murmured. "They're in it together?"

Lila twisted a lock of her hair until it cinched tight around her finger. "Peter does what Harry tells him to. He really thinks his brother is doing something noble, helping his clients get their organs quickly, unlike what happened to Harry's wife."

"And Tank," Angela said. "He was offered money for his kidney, too, wasn't he?"

"He was in trouble. He'd been jailed and he lost his job, lost the money he'd been saving to buy a house. I didn't want to draw his blood in the first place, but Peter insisted. Tank agreed to the surgery, but then he changed his mind. He wanted to go to the police. He begged me to help."

"And that's why your car was blown up. To persuade you not to cooperate."

Her mouth tightened. "Harry will kill anyone who gets in his way. I think he has a bug on my phone. I told Tank I was going to find Ralph Pickford and have him come with me to the police. Harry found out. He got there first. Poor Ralph."

"Yes," Angela said. "Harry has a lot of victims. You and Tank, Cora. What about your son? That's why you're afraid, isn't it? It was Harry who sent the lock of hair in the bouquet of flowers."

She grabbed the handle of her bag and reached for the car door. "I'm out. I'm not going to let my son get hurt. Tell Tank I tried my best. I really did want to do the right thing."

"Is Tank in love with you, Lila?"

She laughed. "No. I loved his brother, Julio."

Angela flinched at the name.

"Tank's tried to help because he knew Julio loved me, too. Mrs. Guzman never wanted me and Julio to be together. She hates me. She wouldn't lift a finger to help me."

"So instead you threw in with the Grubers." Dan figured he probably shouldn't have said it, but it was too late.

"Harry helped me through school, paid my way. Set me up to work with Peter in the clinic. I thought it was kindness, but it was manipulation. Harry was just using me because he knew I'd keep quiet about the blood draws."

"We can help you get out of this mess," Dan said. "Go to the police." Even as he said it he wondered how deeply Lieutenant Torrey was involved. Did he know that Patricia was performing the illegal surgeries? His gut sank as the final piece clicked into place. "Wait a minute. Harry is blackmailing Dr. Lane into doing the surgeries in exchange for getting Lance a kidney, isn't he?"

"I don't know anything about that."

"I think you do."

"I'm leaving," she tossed out.

"You can't just run away, Lila," Angela said.

"Watch me," she said. Before Angela could reach for her wrist, Lila was out the door and hurrying down a side street.

Dan gripped the steering wheel. "Harry isn't going to let her go, and I'm not sure the police will protect her even if we go to them. Lila's in over her head."

"I wonder if we are, too," Angela said. "We can't force Betty to come forward. She would be too fearful anyway, after what happened to Ralph. Tank and Cora have skipped town. What's left to do?"

He had a sinking feeling. "You're right. This is a matter for the police now. You can walk away. You've done your best for Tank." He felt a twist in his heart as he said it. *Walk away.* Walk out of his life. Why did the thought cut at him? The light gilded her hair, tinting her gaze with an even deeper shade of emerald. He smiled, and she shot him a questioning glance.

"I was just thinking about us playing basketball together in Afghanistan."

"Feels like a lifetime ago."

"It was. We were different people then, but I guess that's God's way of growing us up." He gazed out the window as the setting sun painted the sky with pearls and grays. "You know, those were the most intense moments of my life, and some were horrible, but I'd do it all again in a heartbeat."

She was still for a moment. "Crazy as it sounds, even though I will never be free of the horrors, I think I would do it again, too." She smiled. "There was great joy in serving, wasn't there?"

"Yes, there was." And then he was leaning over, stroking her hair and gazing into those incredible eyes. His mouth searched for hers. One moment he felt the warmth of her lips on his, sweet and sincere; then she pulled away sharply.

"I…" he started. "I'm sorry."

"It's not you," she said. "You're an amazing man. And in other circumstances—"

"I understand," he said firmly. "I shouldn't have done that." *Idiot, Dan. Stupid.* She didn't want a relationship, wasn't in the mental frame of mind to welcome one. And he wasn't, either.

She took his hand. "It's okay. We have a connection, don't we? A deep one."

Urgency roiled through him, a thrilling idea and hope. "Do you think someday?"

Color flooded her face. "I can't, Dan. I've got PTSD and it's out of control. I realize that I cannot keep avoiding that. I've got to get some help. That has to be my priority. I don't know if I will ever get past it."

"You will," he said. "I know you will. We could do it together."

"No. I have to get medical help and find a way to restore my connection with the Lord. That has to be first in my life. You helped me start on that journey, and I'll always be grateful for that."

"I see." And he did, at least his brain understood, but his heart was thudding uncomfortably. He heard the finality in her voice. She would leave, and it would be permanent. "So what's next then? For the case, I mean?"

"I can talk to the police in Coronado, since we can't trust Torrey. They'll help me with the investigation. I'll phone my sister Candace back at the office and she can start the ball rolling."

He nodded. "Okay. I guess that's settled then."

"I guess it is. When Donna and Marco make it back, we'll head home." She put her hand out suddenly, fingers trailing along his arm. "I want to say thank you for all that you've gone through to help me."

"Anytime, Sherlock." He forced a grin, then started the car to break the awkwardness. "I'll take you back to the hotel. Marco and Donna will be there soon."

"I need to make another stop first." Something anguished crept into her tone. She laced her fingers together on her lap. "I have to talk to Tank's mom before I leave."

"Are you sure you want to do that?"

She tilted up her chin and nodded once.

"All right." He put the car into drive and started off on what was likely going to be the last leg of their journey together.

Angela experienced a cascade of feelings as they drove to Mrs. Guzman's assisted living facility. There was an ache in her heart from knowing that Dan cared for her so much that he wanted to pursue a relationship, and the pain at knowing she was turning her back on a possible future with him. But there was also a gleam of hope, that somehow, out of the tumultuous last year of her life, God was bringing her closer to Him. He would use her PTSD, her time with Dan and her sisters to bind her heart to His. It would be a painful process, fraught with desperation, but the tiny flame of hope kept flickering inside. God would help her find healing, reconnecting the vine and the branches as they were meant to be.

She got out of the car on shaky legs. What would it be like to face Mrs. Guzman and tell her she was the reason Julio Guzman was dead? Her palms were icy as they entered the lobby and checked in with the nurse. "You'll have to wait a few moments," she said. "Mrs. Guzman is taking some medicine right now. Have a seat for just a minute."

They walked to the serviceable upholstered chairs, next to the windows that overlapped the parking lot. Then she saw him. Tank walked across the lot, his hands shoved into his pockets, head down as if in thought.

Angela was out the door in a moment. "Tank," she said, running to him.

He started, tensed and then relaxed. "Hey."

Dan jogged up behind them. "Thought you were on your way to Mexico."

"I am. Cora is already there. I had to tell my mom I'd be gone for a while." His face crumpled. "She's upset. She doesn't understand that I have to do this to keep Cora safe. I had to keep things vague, you know?"

"We know about Gruber's transplant scheme," Angela said.

Tank's eyes widened. "Now you see what kind of a man he is. I changed my mind about handing over my kidney, and he's been threatening me ever since. When I tried to bring you in to get some evidence…" Tank sighed. "I thought I could make things right. I'm sorry I involved you."

"We are going to get the proof," Dan said. "But if you and Lila went to the cops—"

"The cops?" He shook his head. "I've learned my

lesson. Torrey wants me to turn myself in because he needs my kidney for his son. He's not going to protect me from Gruber. He's going to hand me over, and they'll probably take both my kidneys while they're at it. Now that Lila's running, too, and Ralph Pickford is nearly dead, there's no one to prove what Gruber's been up to."

"But—" Angela started.

He held up a hand. "I'm leaving, but as long as you're here, I got something to say." He shot her a quick look and rubbed a hand across his face. "My brother thought the world of you, Chaplain, and I gotta say he was right. You put yourself on the line for me and Cora, and I can see why Julio did the same for you."

Angela felt the burn of tears as she took the hand he offered. It was a precious sentiment, one that could not come from anyone else but this man, Julio's brother. "Thank you," she whispered.

He shrugged. "My brother was my hero, and I'd do anything for him. I wish I could have told him that once before it was too late."

"He knew," she found herself saying. "He told me all the time about you. He loved you, too."

Tank's mouth twisted in a smile. Then he straightened, looking at his phone. The color ebbed from his face. "Oh, no."

"What is it?" Dan said. "What's wrong?"

Tank gulped. He looked from his phone to them. "Gruber's won," he groaned.

"Tank, what is it?" she said, gripping his hand.

"I have to go."

"Go where?"

His eyes were dull and defeated. "I have to find Harry Gruber and give him what he wants."

"No," she said, clutching his hand.

He smiled at her. "Got no choice. I guess it's my turn to be the hero."

In a moment he'd jerked his hand free and sprinted away.

TWENTY-ONE

While Dan was trying to decide if he should wrestle Tank to the ground and prevent him from leaving or try to talk some sense into the guy, Tank charged out of the lot. Dan nearly caught up, but as he closed in Tank whirled around and punched. The blow connected solidly with Dan's cheekbone, snapping his head back and sending him over backward. As he hit the asphalt, Dan glimpsed Tank sprinting across an intersection.

Dan was getting to his feet when Angela caught up. He winced, his left eye pulsing with the first throb of pain.

She offered a hand. "You're going to have a shiner."

"Sucker punch." Dan got up unassisted.

She scanned the street for any sign of him. "What made him act like that?"

"I wish I knew. Maybe he got word that something happened to Cora."

They jogged back to Dan's truck just as Marco

pulled up, Donna in the passenger seat, craning to see. "Was that Tank we just saw running?" she said. "What happened to your eye?"

Marco grinned. "Looks like he took a left hook."

Dan glowered. "He surprised me, and he's going to pay for it when I catch up with him."

"Just like two boys on a school play yard," Donna said.

"No. We're gonna glove up and I'll flatten him properly in the ring," Dan snapped.

"Let me know if you need some pointers," Marco said.

"I can handle it myself, thanks," Dan huffed. "Can we focus on the bigger picture here? Tank's going to hand himself over to Gruber. Gruber wants his kidney."

Donna gasped. "So that's Gruber's racket. Organ harvesting?"

Angela nodded.

"We'll see if we can run him down before he does something stupid," Marco said. "He's heading west."

"We'll check the clinic and his house." Dan opened the passenger door for Angela, and she climbed in.

With a nod, Marco drove off.

"Okay," Dan said. "You want to talk to Mrs. Guzman before we go?"

She shook her head thoughtfully. "If we don't figure out where Tank was headed, she might be about to lose her second son."

Dan did not answer, but he had the uncomfortable churning in his gut that made him want to agree. He pushed the car faster than the speed limit and they made it to the clinic, where there was no sign of Tank or anyone else. The parking lot was empty, the sun mellowing into dusk. His cheekbone throbbed.

Angela chewed her lip. "Did he go back to his house first?"

They drove there next, but the house was still and quiet. There was no answer to their forceful knocking.

"The hospital?"

Dan shook his head. "I don't think Patricia would want to risk Tank talking to her there. Too public." Yet to remove his kidney, she would have to have access to a surgical room with the necessary equipment, and a nurse to assist. She could not manage that in the hospital without attracting attention." He felt Angela's questioning glance. "She has a place to do all this secretly. And after she's removed the kidney, she'd need to transplant it quickly into Lance before it's no longer viable. Where could she…" The thought struck him like a hammer blow. He wheeled the car in a tight turn, tires squealing.

Angela clutched the door. "What?"

"Underground. That has to be it. The clinic basement."

"But how would she get in there with Lance and Tank undetected?"

He floored the gas, and the truck roared back to the clinic. "The clinic was a library at one time, remember? And the hospital was an old college campus. It was replaced years ago with something much more high tech, but the infrastructure still remains. There must have been a system to move books back and forth as needed between the two buildings before the college built their own library."

He handed her his phone. "Get Jeb on the speakerphone. He's in my contact list."

She did, and, in a moment, Jeb was on the line.

"Is there a connecting tunnel between the hospital and the clinic?" Dan demanded.

Jeb snorted. "Most people start with a hello."

"Urgent, Jeb. What do you know about it?"

"I knew a student who researched the whole thing when he was working on his thesis. Most of the tunnels were filled in."

Dan's stomach plummeted. *Wrong.* He'd been off the mark, a doctor, not a detective.

"But two decades ago there was an underground passage that connected what used to be Cobalt College with the Cobalt Library, which is now the clinic."

Angela leaned forward. "Is there any way that passage still exists?"

"Not sure. I can phone the kid who did the paper and ask." He hesitated. "Funny thing, you bringing this up."

"Why funny?"

"The kid mentioned that he'd worked for Harry Gruber's trucking company while he went to school part-time about a year and a half ago, before Harry started the clinic. Harry was real interested in his research, the kid said. Said he wanted to buy a building that had some history to it."

Dan's mouth went dry. "Can you call him and find out where the access point is on the hospital grounds?"

"Sure. When?"

"Now," Dan said. "Right now."

He could practically hear Angela's mind spinning as he pulled up at the hospital.

"So Dr. Lane moves her equipment and patients via the tunnel to the clinic so she can keep the surgeries secret and care for the patients after the fact."

"I think so, which means that she has some medical people helping her."

"Plus Torrey."

"He's a cop. How far would he go to keep this a secret?" Their eyes met, and she answered her own question. "He'd do anything to make sure his son will get his kidney."

"Anything," Dan agreed.

"If Tank called Dr. Lane, or Gruber himself, he may already be at the clinic or on his way."

They waited an interminable thirty minutes until the phone buzzed.

"Kid says the passage is attached to the unused

utility building on the northeast corner of the property. That help?"

"Sure does. Thanks, Jeb."

"Don't suppose you need the help of an old man and his dog?"

"We could use a lookout," Angela piped up.

"On my way," he said.

Marco and Donna joined them in the hospital parking lot. They started on foot across the darkened hospital property. The utility building was locked at every door.

Angela smacked her hand on her thigh in frustration. "We've got to get in there."

"Would this help?" Jeb smiled, holding up a set of keys as Pogo scampered over to give them all a sniff.

Angela grinned. "You're amazing, Jeb."

"Nah. I just happen to know Norm. He's the oldest janitor on the hospital staff. He's been here for fifty years and he's got keys to everything. Guy never throws anything away."

"I owe you one," Dan said. "Would you stay here, out of sight, and text me if anyone comes this way?"

Jeb beamed. "Yes, indeed. This is the most excitement I've had in decades. But Dan—" he gave him a stern nod "—try to remember that you're a doctor, not a superhero, huh?"

"What do you mean? I've got a cape and everything," he said.

They let themselves into the utility building and began their search.

"Here," Marco called, pointing to a metal door on the far side of the building. "It's this one. Locked."

Dan tried all the keys on the ring until one slid home. "Gonna have to buy Norm a cup of coffee." Pulling the door open, they were hit with a stale smell and silence.

"All right," Marco said. "Donna and Angela—"

"Are not going to wait here while you manly men search, so don't even suggest it," Donna said, arms folded.

Dan shook his head. "We know too much about Gruber. He's got a great reason to kill us."

Angela's determined expression, mirrored on her sister's face, did not change. "I'm going in there to help Tank. I've got to."

A woman with a mission. He saw fear in her eyes, glimmering there like a star about to fall. And that was courage, he thought with a tightening in his chest, to go forward through the fear, holding tight to faith and pressing on. Courage. He gripped her hand.

"If you're sure," he said.

"I haven't been sure of anything since Afghanistan, but this time I'm certain."

He raised her hand to his lips and pressed a kiss there. It was the closest she'd allow, the only way he could savor the fleeting connection between them. When he let her go, his body and soul grieved the loss. "All right," he said, after a breath. "Let's do this."

Angela wished she could have kept hold of Dan's hand as they headed into the passageway. Her imagination had conjured up a rough earthen tunnel, but this was a neatly tiled corridor with plastered walls and bare electric bulbs hanging from the ceiling every six feet or so. They decided to leave the lights off. Except for their phone flashlights, they were in darkness.

She tried to keep her breathing normal as the walls boxed her in. The ceiling was high enough that Dan and Marco did not have to duck, but still it felt as if there was an unbearable weight above her, sinking lower every moment.

Breathe and walk. One foot in front of the other.

The air was cold, damp.

Marco who was in the lead, stopped suddenly. He pointed ahead and whispered, "Door ten feet ahead. Light showing."

Light. Had Patricia already had time to get started operating on Tank? It was just under two hours since they'd lost him in the parking lot. Would Tank be able to deliver himself up to her? What had changed his mind? Goose bumps prickled her flesh. And what reason would Patricia Lane have for keeping him alive, a man who could send her, Torrey and Gruber to jail?

Instincts screamed at her to turn back and run the other way, but instead she sped forward, edging through the door after Marco and Dan, her sister right behind her. They emerged into the basement of the clinic. Half of the space was bracketed by sheets of plastic that hung from the ceiling to the floor. Figures moved behind the plastic, eerie blurred shapes dressed in white.

Dan was already moving, throwing a section of the plastic aside, striding in as they scurried to keep up. Patricia gasped, eyes enormous, dropping a surgical instrument on the floor of the makeshift sterile room. Violet, the nurse from the hospital, heaved a sigh as though she'd been expecting their untimely arrival. Tank lay on a table, eyes half-closed, wearing a hospital gown.

"What…what are you doing here?" Patricia said.

"Stopping you from taking his kidney," Angela said, running to Tank's side and shaking his shoulders. "Wake up, Tank. You're not going to do this."

"Got to save him…for Julio."

He was babbling. The anesthesia.

Dan shook his head. "Patricia, I understand you're desperate, but this isn't the answer."

"Isn't it?" She pointed to Tank. "This man can save Lance. His kidney will spare my granddaughter from being orphaned. And he'll be fine." Her mouth quivered, voice pleading. "Violet and I have done this many times. It will be fine, and Tank will be paid."

"No, he won't, Patricia," Dan said. "Tank's threatened to go to the police. Gruber isn't going to let him walk out of here."

"That's not true," she whispered.

"It is," he said. "And you are a good doctor deep down. You know you can't do this."

"Yes, she can." Torrey stepped through the plastic, holding a gun on them.

Angela froze, heart pounding.

"Patricia, you're going to take out his kidney for Lance, just like we've been planning for months. I'll make sure Gruber doesn't kill Tank. It's time to help our own."

Marco shifted back slightly. Donna drew closer to Angela. Dan must have read Marco's intent. He took a step toward Torrey. "So you see how this is spinning out of control, Patricia? He's pulled a gun on us. There are four of us here who know the truth, plus Tank and Lila. Six people. Are you going to kill us all, Torrey? Because I'm pretty sure one of us can get you before Patricia takes out Tank's kidney."

Torrey's grip on the gun tightened. "I know there's nothing left for me. I'm over as a cop. All I can do now is make sure Lance gets what he needs. He hates me, anyway, so he won't cry when I go to jail. At least I'll know I saved his life and his kid will have a daddy."

Marco slowly reached out a hand toward a small wheeled table. A few inches more and he'd have it.

"But she's a doctor," Dan said. "Do no harm. Tank doesn't want this."

"Sure he does. Came on his own, didn't he?"

"What did Gruber threaten him with?" Angela said, rewarded when Torrey's attention shifted slightly to her. "He was ready to flee the country and then all of a sudden he's here handing over his kidney?"

"Don't know. Don't care. I only—"

Marco made his move, shoving the rolling cart, which shot forward and clipped Torrey in the knee. He reeled backward, and both Marco and Dan were on top of him. Fists and feet slammed into the rolling cart, the operating table, the lamp, scattering utensils. The metal tools clanged to the ground.

Torrey thrashed, refusing to relinquish his grip on the gun.

It seemed as though Marco had secured his wrist when he kneed him in the chest. Dan dove for his arm as the door to the basement room slammed open. Lila staggered in, face ghastly pale, shrieking.

"Where is he? Where's—" She did not get out the last word as Torrey's gun fired.

Angela screamed as the shot exploded through the space. Lila tumbled backward, crashed against the door frame and crumpled to the floor.

Marco snapped out a fist and dealt Torrey a blow to the jaw that knocked him unconscious. While Donna secured the gun, Marco found a roll of duct tape to secure the officer's hands behind him. Patricia dropped to her knees next to Lila, where Dan was already crouched.

"Wound to her leg. Superficial," he said. "The fall knocked her out."

Violet grabbed a handful of gauze and pressed it to Lila's injury.

Dan shot her a look.

"I needed the money, Dr. Blackwater," Violet said. "We believed all the patients were willing participants. But I'm still a nurse, no matter what you think of me."

Angela sucked in a shaky breath. It could have been worse. So much worse. She went to Tank, shaking him gently, trying to wake him up. Across the room a flash of movement caught her eye. For one moment, Harry Gruber peered through the partially opened stairwell door, face contorted in anger. Before the door slammed shut, she heard a sound that froze her blood.

A cry. A tiny wail. A baby.

Tank's words echoed in her memory. *Got to save him...for Julio.*

Breath stopped, she looked at Lila, understanding at last why Tank had handed himself over. Then she was running for the stairs.

Donna screamed, "Angela, no."

But she did not hear. There was only one thought in her mind now.

Save Lila's baby.

Julio's son.

TWENTY-TWO

She slammed against the panic bar and raced up the basement steps, taking them two at a time. The baby's cries were louder now.

"Stop," she screamed at Gruber, filled with a fury she could not contain. A baby. A helpless innocent. How dare he use him like a chess piece to get Tank to deliver himself up. With Tank's wife safely in Mexico, Gruber knew the only choice was to threaten Quinn. Lila must have revealed the truth to Tank, that the child was Julio's.

Gruber pounded up the steps ahead of her, one flight, two. He was huffing; she could hear his rasping pants. Her own legs were cramping from the effort. Where was he headed? She heard keys scrabbling on metal as he unlocked the stairwell door.

He'd banged through, and she was after him in a moment, void of any kind of a plan except to get that child out of his arms. Close now, she was only a few feet away from him. Behind her she heard the door shut, locked from the outside as it was when they'd encountered Peter Gruber. Darkness made her pause, her eyes adjusting. She could hear Harry's feet scuffing over the tile now, loud in the darkened office. Easing forward, she emerged into the examination area and stopped so suddenly her feet squeaked on the tile. No movement. Was he behind one of the partitions, waiting to attack her as she went by?

She recalled the feel of his knife on her back, the numbing terror she'd felt as he held her down, the bullets screaming at her past the lighthouse when he'd terrorized her then. *Not this time*, she decided. *I'm going to protect that baby.* One foot in front of the other. She crept forward another step, ears straining.

Where was he? The sounds were distorted by the cubicle walls, a clock ticking, muffled shouts from somewhere below, the wild thumping of her own pulse nearly drowning out everything else.

The groan of wood and metal jerked her attention to the back wall. Gruber heaved open the window with one hand and stepped out onto the fire escape. That's why he'd run to the second floor. He intended to escape down the ladder since the police might very well be entering through the front door. Sprinting forward, she was at the open window in a moment.

"You're not getting away," she said. "Not with that baby."

He stopped, hands under the squirming baby's arms as if he were some detestable thing Harry could not bear to hold close. Slowly he turned to look at her, beads of sweat dancing on his forehead. "You're right," he said, a smile lighting his face. "Not with the baby."

In horror she watched him grab the back of the baby's jumper with one hand and dangle him over the railing.

"No," she shouted, lunging forward.

He swung the baby farther out, stopping her progress with an upturned palm.

Quinn pinwheeled his plump arms and legs, wailing, head lolling on his delicate neck.

"Don't," she said. "You'll hurt him. Please stop."

He smiled. "And now we're at the point where the rubber meets the road, Detective. Or do you go by Chaplain these days?"

"You're finished. There's no way out. Too many people know about your organ harvesting. Lila will tell everything to the police when she comes to, and so will Tank."

"Ingrates," he muttered. "They were happy to cooperate when it benefited them. Now they go all high-and-mighty when things get dicey."

"There's no reason to hurt the baby and make things worse for yourself."

"No reason?" His lips twitched, the smile gone. "How about simple justifiable anger? My plans are spoiled, plans that I labored over and poured money into. Why should Lila get to enjoy her little brat when I won't be able to dote on my grandkids like I'd planned? I helped Lila with school. Rent. I kept the money coming her way, and what do I get out of it?"

"You manipulated her into breaking the law."

"The law?" His laugh was bitter. "You know what, Chaplain? There's a higher law. Shouldn't you know that from your Bible teaching? Saving lives is the greater moral law, isn't it?"

"You've lined your pockets from your illegal organ harvesting. Don't try to pretend it's some noble calling. You did it for money, pure and simple."

"It was a win-win. I saved many lives by providing organs instead of making people wait until it was too late. But it's too late to save Lance Torrey. Now that you've wrecked my setup, he's going to die waiting for a kidney. His death is on your conscience, just like Tank's brother. What was his name again? Julio, wasn't it?"

The name struck at her. She blinked. Another death laid at her feet? Guilt rose dark and thick. She shifted.

"Yes, Guzman jumped in front of a bullet that was meant for you. How do you live with yourself knowing that?"

She took a deep breath, reaching deep down past the guilt and the horror, to a memory of his smile, his pride in the job he was doing, his service to others. "Julio Guzman sacrificed himself to save me. It was tragic, and I will carry that with me forever, but I won't blame myself anymore." It filled her with invisible strength to say the words out loud. God had lifted her out of the pit, she realized in that moment. It was still dark, frightening and far from over, perhaps it never would be, but she had hope that she was reconnected to the vine.

Fists pounded on the stairwell door, which had locked behind her. She pictured Dan, Marco and Donna hammering against it, desperate to help. But there would be no help. Not in time. Not from them.

"Harry, give me the baby," she said, voice icy calm.

"I don't think so. I'll tell you what's going to happen here," Gruber said. "I'm going to climb down this fire escape and disappear, and you're going to let me."

"I'm not."

He lowered his arm suddenly. The baby swung wildly, head jostling to and fro. Quinn wailed, face red where the collar of his clothing was cinched tight against his throat.

She stifled the urge to scream.

"My hand is getting awful sweaty," Gruber said, jerking the baby around.

She switched strategies. "You don't want to hurt this child, Harry. You love children. I know how much you love your own grandchildren, right?"

"I do love my grandchildren." He looked at the

dangling baby as if he hadn't noticed him before. She felt a swell of hope. If she could just get him to put Quinn down.

"But I couldn't care less about this specimen." He swung the baby again, and Angela couldn't hold back.

"No," she screamed.

Gruber laughed. "Tell you what. I'm not an unreasonable man. Let's trade."

"Trade?" Her heart tightened with each movement of his arm, each infant gasp and cough.

"Sure," Gruber said. "I'll take you as a hostage and leave Baby Snookums here. How's that sound? You'll come with me until I get to the airport, and then I'll let you go."

She did not believe him for a moment, but she had to get the baby back inside to safety. Body prickling in terror, she nodded. "I will come with you. Just hand me the baby before he falls."

He gave one last smile and then lurched. The baby cried out, and Angela gasped, impulsively making a grab. Harry laughed at his pretense. "You're so easy to fool. Here. If you want this screaming brat, take him."

Angela reached out through the window, snatching hold of the baby and pulling him close before Harry changed his mind. Quinn was rigid with fear, nearly unable to breathe through his choking wails.

"It's okay, sweetie," she murmured over the wild

thumping of her own heart. "We'll get you to your mama real soon."

"You know what?" Harry said, staring calculatingly at her. "I've reconsidered."

She backed away, turning sideways to shield the baby. She'd have to run for the door if he came for them. She imagined what it would feel like to be shot in the back. Goose bumps prickled her flesh. "I'll go with you, just like you said."

"Angela," Dan hollered. Dan and Marco must have split up. She could hear Dan coming closer, racing up the interior stairs now while the others continued to slam against the door, which vibrated from the blows. A piece of the door frame splintered off and plunked to the floor.

"Nah," Harry said thoughtfully. "I've decided a hostage would just slow me down."

"We had a deal."

He smiled. "Like I said, you're so easy to fool."

He fired.

Angela did not feel pain when the bullet struck her side, blowing her off her feet. Her only thought was to keep the baby from hitting the floor. She clutched him to her as she fell.

Fragments of thought shot through her brain. The baby. Julio's baby. She summoned up her only remaining strength. "Father God," she breathed, "save Julio's son."

As her eyes closed, the last thing she felt was

Quinn's tiny hand on her cheek, whisper-soft fingertips searching for comfort she could not give.

Dan cleared the top step, the echo of the gunshot rocketing through his senses, twining together with another sound that made no sense, the crying of an infant. The shock caused him to stop dead in his tracks.

Angela lay on her side, body curled around Lila's son. They were both very still, silent. For a moment, he could not move. This could not be the end, not for Lila's baby, not for Angela. Horror choked off his breath, stunning him like a grenade blast.

Move, he commanded his body. For a moment he found his muscles would not obey. The outer stairwell door burst open as Marco kicked it down.

"Gruber," he shouted, running to the window and clattering down the ladder.

Donna ran after Marco, stopping short when she saw what lay on the floor. Her mouth opened, eyes beyond anguished.

Her cry startled Dan into action. He leaped forward, sinking to his knees next to Angela, fingers reaching first for the child. Cold shuddered through him. For all his cases in Afghanistan, those burrowed most painfully in his memories were the children. Caught in the cross fire of enemies they did not know, steeped in poverty they could not overcome, they were the most undeserving of their cruel injuries. He forced out his fingers to stroke the baby's cheek.

The boy flung up an arm, starting up a healthy wail that flooded Dan with deep relief. He extricated him from Angela's grasp and handed him to Donna.

"Check him for bleeding."

She gently put him on the floor as she examined him. "No sign of blood. He's breathing and crying. I don't see any wounds of any kind." Donna picked him up and began to gently rock him, eyes riveted on her sister. "Oh, Dan. Is she…"

Marco raced in. "Cops got him at the bottom—" He broke off and raced to Angela.

Until that moment, Dan was not completely certain of his God-given purpose. Was it to resume his career as a doctor knowing that there would be more names to add to his notebook, names of people he could not save? Or walk away and enjoy the life of easier pursuits that did not cost him a piece of himself each time another heart stopped under his care? He'd done his time, for sure, encountering more loss and carnage than any surgeon should witness in a lifetime.

Yet as he looked at Angela, blood staining the hem of her shirt, helpless, hopeless to aid herself, his purpose recrystallized inside him, strong and sure as it ever was. He hesitated no longer. Checking quickly for breathing and a pulse, he found both. A quick exam showed that the bullet struck her in the ribs, plowing its way inside with no exit wound that he could find. There was no telling how much internal injury had occurred as the metal drove through her insides. Marco was already on the phone demanding an ambulance.

It was on him to keep her steady, stable until they got there. She was strong; she had so many reasons to survive. *You're going to live, Angela.* Then he heard the soft whoosh of air, and his body went rigid as she began to gasp, her face gone deadly pale.

"Get my bag," he yelled, pointing. "Corner desk on the shelf."

Both Donna and Marco sprinted toward his cubicle. Marco returned in seconds, putting the bag next to him. "What?"

"Traumatic pneumothorax." Dan yanked open the bag.

"English," Donna pleaded.

"The bullet hole is causing her chest cavity to fill with air. The pressure is going to collapse her lung if we don't stop it."

"How? Her lips are turning blue," Donna said in horror. "Do something."

Though he did not have a kit specially designed for the task, he handed Marco a plastic bag full of cotton balls while he pawed frantically through his supplies for tape.

"Cotton balls?" Marco said. "How's that gonna help?"

"Dump them out. We need the bag."

Marco did, and Dan cut off a strip of tape. "Hold this."

Dan placed the bag over the wound and taped down one side.

"More tape."

Marco peeled off another strip. By the time he'd secured it on three sides they heard the sirens.

Dan stopped him from cutting another strip of tape. "It's sealed for now. No more air will get in. We'll leave one edge open so hopefully some air can escape," he said, while checking her pulse again. Her lips were still bluish, but her breathing was slightly improved, he thought. Or was it what he wanted to think?

He brushed the hair from her face. Knowing all the terrible scenarios that could take place as a result of a gunshot wound made him crazy. Was she bleeding internally right now? Her life ebbing away and him powerless to stop it?

No, not powerless. Dan Blackwater would never be powerless because he worked for the Great Physician, the one who'd healed Dan and would heal Angela in this world or the next. God had been that presence through every surgery, stilling Dan's hands, sustaining his strength, protecting his mind. God was in the adrenaline-fueled moments when he'd triumphed and the sweat-soaked instances when he'd not. And He was here now with Dan, the connection strong as it ever had been.

He knelt very close so his mouth was next to her

ear, the silky strands of her hair tickling him. "Hey, Angela," he whispered. "You're going to be okay, and I'm going to stay with you and make sure." He kissed her cheek and laid his face next to hers, listening to the ebb and flow of each precious God-given breath. And then he began to pray.

TWENTY-THREE

Angela drifted in and out of consciousness for the next several days after the surgery to remove the bullet and repair the damage. It was a surreal time. Her mother was there; Sarah and Candace, Marco and Donna were never far away. She'd ascertained that baby Quinn was unharmed, returned to healing Lila, who was getting help from Tank and the newly returned Cora. This time when she forced her eyes open, it was Dan smiling down at her.

"Hey there, Chaplain. How are you feeling?"

She sighed. "Like I've been run over by a train."

He laughed.

"I've been wondering about Peter."

"He's being charged, as well. He will be in jail along with his brother.

"Case closed," she said, staring at him. "You're wearing your doctor's coat."

"Yes, ma'am. I've returned to my duties. The hospital's down a doctor and a nurse."

"Will Dr. Lane and Violet go to jail, too?"

"At least for a while."

"And Torrey?"

"Definitely Torrey. There's some good news. I understand Lance has entered an alcohol treatment program so the OTPN is reviewing his case again."

"Can you influence them? He's the only parent to a little girl, and now her grandparents are going to be in jail."

"I will put in my two cents—we'll see where that takes us." He took her hand. "And what about you?" His eyes were dark and soft. "Won't be long before you're released. What's your plan?"

She understood what he really wanted to know. Was there room in her future for him? She pressed his hand to her cheek for a moment. "I'm so grateful to you for everything you've done for me—really I am."

"But you're going home and not planning on returning to Cobalt Cove anytime soon?"

Her throat thickened. "I've got to go back. I have to heal, get help. Most of all, I need to find out if I can be a chaplain again."

He gave a slow nod. "And you're not looking for friendly visitors."

"I'm sorry, Dan. I know you care about me. And believe me—I will never forget everything you've done for me." *And I love you*, she wanted to whisper, but the voice was locked inside with all the turmoil and fear and emotional muck she needed to wade through. "You helped me find God again."

"He wasn't ever lost."

"No, but I was. I still am, but you helped me reconnect. It's a tenuous connection right now. I have to strengthen it, and strengthen myself."

He gave her a wry smile. "I'm a patient man, Angela. I can wait."

"Why would you want to?" she said, eyes filling. "I'm a mess, damaged goods. You could have someone else."

He took a breath. "God taught me a lesson in Kandahar. You have to hold on to the blessings in life. Every moment is precious."

"And you'll always be precious to me," she said through the sharp pain in her chest. "I'll never forget you."

"Ditto," he said with a smile that did not quite reach his eyes.

Her heart was still thumping in pain when there was a knock. Dan shot her a look of astonishment as he held open the door for Tank and his mother.

Dan was not sure if he should leave or stay, but he figured Angela might need him in some way. He could not have her in his life, but he could at least look out for her while she was in his hospital. A tingle of pride warmed his insides as he realized he thought of the hospital as his domain again. That part of his life was mercifully clear now. It eased the pain that came with knowing Angela would soon be walking away from him.

Mrs. Guzman sat in a wheelchair, brown hair shot with gray. He was surprised to note that she held Quinn in her arms. Lila walked in with them, using a cane for support. She looked tired but peaceful somehow.

Tank cleared his throat. "We're sorry to intrude, but my mother wanted to come talk to you."

The baby squirmed, and Mrs. Guzman soothed him expertly, face softening as she adjusted his blanket with her arthritic hands. "You served with my son," she said, voice clipped, heavily accented.

Angela's cheeks paled. "Yes, ma'am. Julio was a fine man and a fine soldier."

Her lips thinned into a tight line. "They told me he died protecting you."

He heard Angela swallow hard. "Yes, he did."

"I was angry. I felt that you should not have lived when my son did not."

Dan wanted to blurt out something, anything to ease the stricken look on Angela's face, but he knew this was her moment to speak, a moment that might change the course of her healing and her life.

Angela sat up a little higher on the pillows, fingers clutched on the blanket. "I felt that way, too, for a long time, Mrs. Guzman, and sometimes I still do. I am so sorry." Tears streamed down her face. "I can never express how sorry I am."

Mrs. Guzman cocked her head slightly. "Julio wrote me letters. I have them in a box that belonged to his father. Julio said that you were over there risking yourself to take care of other people in your own way, like he was in his. What does that mean?"

"I was…I am a navy chaplain. I went to minister."

I am… Dan thrilled at the words.

Mrs. Guzman shifted. "And George—"

Tank blushed at the use of his proper name. "Everyone calls me Tank, Mama."

"That is no kind of a name," she said, fixing him with a look before she again turned to Angela, fingers stroking the baby's hand. "George told me you risked yourself for this baby, my grandson, and for Lila." She glanced at Lila. "They were married, Lila and Julio. Secretly, when he was on leave. They did not tell me because they knew I would not approve." Her eyes were filled with regret.

Angela stayed quiet.

"I didn't know I had a grandson until Lila brought him to me a few days ago." Her gaze dropped to the baby, and she stared at him in wonder. "I hated you. And Lila. I tried to keep Lila way from Julio because I thought she wasn't good for him." Her mouth quivered. "I have asked Lila to forgive me." Dan noticed then the dog tags, Julio's, hanging around Lila's neck. Mrs. Guzman must have given them to her. There was no greater sign of reconciliation than that.

Dan's spirit lifted. Quinn would know his grandmother, his uncle, his family. *Thank You, Lord.*

But there was still more forgiveness that needed to happen.

Mrs. Guzman cleared her throat. "On his last visit home, my Julio wouldn't stay with me because he knew I would speak ill about Lila. I lost those days with my son as a punishment for my hatred. I lost all these months with my grandson, too. My heart has been so hard, a sinner's heart." She blinked, moisture sparkling in her eyes.

"I know what it's like to have regrets, Mrs. Guzman. Believe me," Angela said softly. "You loved your son and he knew that. He told me often. He would be so happy to know that you and Lila have made amends."

"We will be a family now, like Julio would have wanted." Mrs. Guzman's mouth quivered as she stared at Angela. "I am glad my son was serving next to you. And I am grateful that you saved my grandson and brought me a daughter to love."

Lila reached out and touched Mrs. Guzman's shoulder. Carefully, without disturbing the baby, Julio's mother covered the young woman's hand with hers.

"Thank you," Mrs. Guzman said one final time, her faded eyes wet with moisture. She spoke to Tank in Spanish, and he wheeled her out of the room. Lila stopped to give Angela a kiss.

"Thank you for saving my son," Lila said. She left, and the door closed behind them.

Dan looked at Angela, who sat stone still, staring at the door.

"Are you all right?" he said after a beat.

She gulped. "Not yet, but finally I think I'm going to be."

He held her hand and pressed it to his cheek, silently thanking God for the amazing event he'd been privileged to witness.

"I'm going to miss you," she said, "when they let me out of here."

"Me, too," he said.

Her eyes met his, and the words tumbled out, straight from his heart.

"I love you, Angela. It's selfish to say that when you can't return the feeling, I know. I'm sorry, but I have to say it before you leave me."

"Dan—"

He stopped her, kissing her fingertips. "I'm not expecting you to say anything at all." Anguish and love, triumph and torment rolled around together in his body. "I just want you to know that I will be praying for you, every day, unceasingly."

He looked into those rich green eyes one more time, pressed a kiss to her cheek and walked away, forcing himself not to bow against the crushing pain sinking his soul to the depths.

Dr. Dan Blackwater, a man who had repaired countless human hearts, felt his own stutter painfully in his chest.

Goodbye, Angela.
I love you.

Dan watched a young couple giggling as they paddled the tandem kayak in the golden June sunshine, heading toward the slough. The young woman in back, with her ponytail bobbing, splashed water on her companion, who returned the favor, leaving them both laughing. Their easy companionship was evident as they moved lazily through the bay. Dan eased himself down on the bench. His feet hurt from an eight-hour surgery he'd completed earlier in the day. A success, thank the Lord.

He should be exhausted, and physically he was, but his mind would not slip into an easy rhythm. He'd changed into his exercise clothes, thinking maybe a bracing six-mile run might settle him down, but as he sat on the bench he could not shake the sadness at the piece gone missing from his life, a bright-eyed marvel of a woman who did not love him, not enough. He sent up a prayer for Angela, as he did any time she surfaced in his heart.

He lay down on his back on the bench, closing his eyes, letting the sun work its way into his bones. A shadow crept over his vision. He opened an eye.

Silhouetted in luminous splendor was Angela Gallagher, hair flying loose, wearing a denim jacket and khaki capris. He was dreaming, he thought, blinking.

Then she held out a hot dog, slathered with mustard. Odd dream that included hot dogs. A warm drip of mustard plopped down, landing on his cheek. He sat up so fast his head spun.

"Sorry about that." She laughed, wiping away the spot with the heel of her hand. "Good thing I didn't load it with jalapeños."

"Angela?"

"Are you going to take this hot dog or do I need to eat the poor bare thing? I'll do it, even though it's missing a half-dozen condiments."

He took the dog, set it down on the bench and turned to face her. The dark circles were gone from under her eyes; her skin was tanned, body relaxed. His gut hitched tight with the joy of having her so near again. "I'm surprised to see you," he managed. "What brings you to town?"

"I wanted to invite you to a little party my family is having." She blushed. "I'm returning to my chaplain duties, so I guess it's a congratulations party. You were instrumental in that process, so I wanted to invite you personally."

His chest tightened. Gratitude was not the emotion he wanted from her. Why had he let himself hope for more, even for a second? "I'd be honored to come. I'll even put on long pants."

She smiled.

"But you could have sent me a text," he said. "You didn't have to make the drive to Monterey to invite me to a party."

"I wanted to personally invite Lila, Jeb, Tank, Cora and Mrs. Guzman, too."

"Quite a bash you're planning."

"I've been working hard, getting help from a doctor and other chaplains." She offered another smile. "Jeb would be happy to hear I've even been matched with a service puppy."

"That's incredible," he said. "I'm proud of you."

Her cheeks pinked to match the rosy tint of sunset. "And you? Your practice keeping you busy?"

"Yes, in a good way. It's where God means for me to be right now, I think."

For a moment they fell silent, and he sensed she had more to say.

She pulled at the zipper on her jacket. "Healing from PTSD has made me realize a couple of things that I was too foggy to acknowledge before."

"What's that?"

"First off, you really do have pretty awesome hot dogs here in Monterey. I've been having a craving."

He laughed. "All right. One hot dog dinner coming up before you head back home. On me."

"Big spender," she teased.

"Only for you." His tone was light, but his heart infused the words with a deep longing. *Oh, what I would do for you, Angela... Only for you.*

"But mostly I came to Cobalt Cove because I've realized that I'm ready now."

He raised an eyebrow. "For what?"

"For us."

He stood stock still. "What did you say?"

She reached out slowly and took his hand. "I said, for us."

Dumbfounded, he listened to her talk, all the while thinking he must be still in the grip of some sort of dream. She toyed with his fingers.

"Dr. Blackwater, you are an incredible man. A tad on the arrogant side, and you have an irrational fear of rats—"

"It's not irrational—"

She cut him off. "But you are a man of faith, compassion, gentleness, courage and—" she swallowed "—the man that I believe God designed to be my partner in this life… At least, if you want to be."

The pulse pounded in his throat, ringing in his ears. "I can't believe what I'm hearing," he whispered.

She stepped close and held his shoulders. He relished the strength in her fingers, the passion in her eyes. His heart could not understand what his ears were hearing.

"I love you, Dan," she said, voice soft and tender. "I am not fully healed yet, and maybe I never will be, but I can tell you that I've done a lot of praying on the subject and you have never left my heart even for a moment. I…I would like to try to build a life with you, if you still love me, that is." She looked into his face. "Do you still love me, Dan?"

He could stand it no longer. Bending, he kissed her deeply, releasing that stubborn bit of hope that he'd carried, joy fanned to life by the warmth of her kiss and the fresh ocean breeze.

"Angela, I love you so much," he said. "From the moment I saw you in Kandahar, I knew we were meant to be together."

"Sherlock to your Watson?" she whispered, breathless and beaming.

"Mrs. to my Mr.," he said, soul overflowing.

"A chaplain and a doctor," she said, giggling. "Could there be a better pair than that?"

"No way," he said, leaning in for another kiss.

* * * * *

Dear Reader,

This series is near and dear to my heart because the stories take place along my beloved California coast. Here in Northern California we are people who love our outdoors, and folks here are perpetually walking, biking, running, kayaking and swimming. The ocean air is said to be a balm to the soul, but in this story, it takes more than the lovely scenery to heal Angela Gallagher. She struggles with her public persona as a chaplain and her very private battle with PTSD. I hope this story might be of some comfort to those who suffer with the aftermath of trauma in their lives. It is my prayer that you will find a listening ear, a helping hand, and find comfort knowing that God loves you deeply, unconditionally and permanently.

It is always a joy to hear from my readers. If you would like to contact me, feel free to do so via my website at www.danamentink.com. If you prefer to correspond by mail, you can reach me at PO Box 3168, San Ramon, CA, 94583.

God bless.

Dana Mentink

LARGER-PRINT BOOKS!

GET 2 FREE
LARGER-PRINT NOVELS
PLUS 2 FREE
MYSTERY GIFTS

Love Inspired®

Larger-print novels are now available...

LILP15

LARGER-PRINT BOOKS!

GET 2 FREE
LARGER-PRINT NOVELS
PLUS 2 FREE
MYSTERY GIFTS

Love Inspired®
SUSPENSE
RIVETING INSPIRATIONAL ROMANCE

Larger-print novels are now available...

YES! Please send me 2 FREE LARGER-PRINT Love Inspired® Suspense novels and my 2 FREE mystery gifts (gifts are worth about $10). After receiving them, if I don't wish to receive any more books, I can return the shipping statement marked "cancel." If I don't cancel, I will receive 4 brand-new novels every month and be billed just $5.49 per book in the U.S. or $5.99 per book in Canada. That's a savings of at least 19% off the cover price. It's quite a bargain! Shipping and handling is just 50¢ per book in the U.S. and 75¢ per book in Canada.* I understand that accepting the 2 free books and gifts places me under no obligation to buy anything. I can always return a shipment and cancel at any time. Even if I never buy another book, the two free books and gifts are mine to keep forever.

110/310 IDN GH6P

Name	(PLEASE PRINT)
Address	Apt. #
City	State/Prov.	Zip/Postal Code

Signature (if under 18, a parent or guardian must sign)

Mail to the Reader Service:
IN U.S.A.: P.O. Box 1867, Buffalo, NY 14240-1867
IN CANADA: P.O. Box 609, Fort Erie, Ontario L2A 5X3

**Are you a current subscriber to Love Inspired® Suspense books
and want to receive the larger-print edition?
Call 1-800-873-8635 or visit www.ReaderService.com.**

* Terms and prices subject to change without notice. Prices do not include applicable taxes. Sales tax applicable in N.Y. Canadian residents will be charged applicable taxes. Offer not valid in Quebec. This offer is limited to one order per household. Not valid for current subscribers to Love Inspired Suspense larger-print books. All orders subject to credit approval. Credit or debit balances in a customer's account(s) may be offset by any other outstanding balance owed by or to the customer. Please allow 4 to 6 weeks for delivery. Offer available while quantities last.

Your Privacy—The Reader Service is committed to protecting your privacy. Our Privacy Policy is available online at www.ReaderService.com or upon request from the Reader Service.

We make a portion of our mailing list available to reputable third parties that offer products we believe may interest you. If you prefer that we not exchange your name with third parties, or if you wish to clarify or modify your communication preferences, please visit us at www.ReaderService.com/consumerschoice or write to us at Reader Service Preference Service, P.O. Box 9062, Buffalo, NY 14240-9062. Include your complete name and address.

LISLP15